The Alien of Orchard Lake

JIM BATES

www.darkmythpublications.com

Dark Myth Publications, a division of
The JayZoMon/Dark Myth Company, LLC.
21050 Little Beaver Rd, Apple Valley, CA 92308

ISBN: 979-8-9863807-4-2

First Printing December 2022

Dark Myth Publications is a registered trademark of The JayZoMon/Dark Myth Company, LLC.

10 9 8 7 6 5 4 3 2 1

This book is dedicated to my Aunt Barb who has taught me that there is more to life than first meets the eye

Chapter One

EBAR HATED THE feeling the drugs were giving him.

"It's just a little sedative to calm you down," Doctor Franklin had told him when he was first admitted. "Just to help you relax." Then he had turned to the two large, muscle-bound orderlies standing at attention and commanded, "Grab him!" Which they did, holding Ebar's arm tightly while an even larger and more muscle-bound nurse administered the shot. Her name tag read *Freida* but to Ebar it could have easily read *Goliath*. He'd never had someone man-handle him like she did. In moments he was in La La Land.

At the time, being ganged up on by a doctor, two orderlies and a nurse at the Bison County Psychiatric Unit seemed unfair, if not overkill, to the skinny and normally agreeable Ebar. But at four against one, the odds were definitely not in his favor. He had no choice but to give in, and he'd been in La La land ever since, drifting into and out of consciousness for the next three days. And for each and every one of those days, whenever he was conscious, the more Ebar thought about it, the more unfair the whole thing seemed. After all, he'd only gotten into a fight with that idiot, Al. He hadn't tried to start a third world war.

By the fourth day, Ebar was just plain mad. He'd come out of the drug induced fog in his brain and made a snap decision to make a run for it. *Time to get out of here.* He went to sit up to get out of bed but couldn't. He looked down to find his arms and legs were restrained by thick leather straps. *What was going on?* He struggled for a minute, tossing this way and that like a boat on a stormy sea, but got nowhere. Reluctantly, he gave up, lay back and closed his eyes. A memory came to him of a Franz Kafka book he'd read about a guy who had been falsely accused of a crime and slowly went insane trying to cope. Is that what was happening to him?

Panic set in and his heart starting racing, pounding like a drum in his chest. Unwilling to give up, he fought against his rising fear. *Keep it together. You've got to get control of yourself.*

He focused on his breathing, taking deep breaths, in and out, in and out, and after a minute, he felt himself calming down. Good. Whatever was happening, he wasn't going to let them get the better of him. He took another deep breath, let it out and stared at the ceiling. He began counting the perforated holes in the tiles but found he was too preoccupied to keep track of them and quickly lost count, the holes eventually blending together into a gapping morass of nothingness.

He kept going back to the fight at the sewage treatment plant. *So, what if I went a little crazy and beat the living daylights out of Al? I couldn't help it. He had trapped me in the sewer pipe. I could have drowned if I hadn't been able to get out in time. So, what if I beat him up? He had it coming.*

To Ebar's way of thinking, he should have been a hero, but he wasn't. Instead, they'd put him in jail, which, even though he didn't like it, made sense. After all, he *had* gotten into a fight. But then they had decided to send him to the psych ward. Which hadn't made sense. *It's beyond...*

Ebar was going to finish his thought with... *beyond comprehension* when, all of a sudden, the fog in his brain lifted momentarily, and he realized something disquieting. "Oh, no," he mumbled out loud. "I couldn't have...I couldn't have made that kind of a mistake, could I? Nah, no way"

Or could he?

The memory came back with a vengeance. He'd been in jail for assaulting Al. That much was clear. The jailer, a big jerk of a red neck was hassling him, saying, "Hi there, pretty boy. You're going to be someone's nice little meal tonight, aren't you? Oh, I know for a fact that you are." Then he'd puckered up his chapped lips and made smoochy, kissy sounds. It had been disgusting.

Ebar remembered trying to tune the guy out. Instead of listening, he'd closed his eyes and gone into his mind, his safest place of refuge. And while he was in his sanctuary, he traveled back to Rykos, his home planet, and began talking to the man in charge of his mission to earth.

Commander Zenon, are you there? Can he hear me? If you can, you've got to help me. Pease get me out of this horror. I know I shouldn't have beat up Al, but he was messing around with the water supply for Orchard Lake. And you know how much we want that water. Right? One of these days you'll send a mission to earth, and you'll take over the planet and get rid of its inhabitants. Then earth and all of its the water will be ours and..."

Except he'd been so upset with being in jail that he'd made a mistake and forgotten to connect telepathically with his home planet and with commander Zenon. Big mistake. The jerk of a jailer had overheard everything he'd said. Next thing he knew he'd been sent to the Bison County Psychiatric Unit, and his life had gone from being nice, calm, and predictable, to being institutionalized, shot up with drugs and analyzed every waking moment. And probably every sleeping moment, too, for all he knew.

Ebar didn't get scared very often, but now, after four days of institutionalization and now being strapped down like a madman, he was. He tried to turn over, but the restraints held him firm. He lay on his back and closed his eyes and tried to pretend this wasn't happening.

But it was.

He'd never been so frightened in his entire life.

Or alone.

Chapter Two

EBAR MUST HAVE fallen asleep, because the next thing he was aware of was the presence of someone in his room. He dragged himself out of his muddled state of mind and opened his eyes, expecting the two orderlies and the big goliath of a nurse to be encircling his bed preparing to jam another injection into his arm. But it wasn't them, thank goodness. It was his counselor, Jeremy Slater, and Ebar was elated to see him. Even though they'd just met briefly the day before, Ebar had a good feeling about the personable, bearded young man.

Unable to raise a hand in greeting, Ebar cracked a weak smile and said, "Hi Jeremy."

His counselor took one look at the leather straps and shouted, "My god! What's going on with these restraints?"

Ebar shook his head. "I have no idea. I woke up today and there they were. Can you help me?"

"Don't worry. I'm on it right now." Jeremy turned and ran from the room, calling over his shoulder, "Don't go anywhere."

In spite of being hazy due to his medications, Ebar grinned at the statement, relieved that he finally had someone who would help him. He called back, "Don't worry, I won't." But Jeremy was gone, and the sound of his footsteps were already fading as he raced down the hall.

Fifteen minutes later, the restraints had been removed, along with an admonishment from the head nurse. "As long as you're taking his case, Mr. Slater, he can be unrestrained. We just did it for his protection."

"What'd he do to deserve the restraints?" Jeremy asked.

"Well, nothing. Like I said, it's just a precaution."

"Look. You don't have to worry about him, nurse. I'll take full responsibility."

She looked at him skeptically. "Well, okay, then. If you say so."

"Good. Because I do say so."

Ebar watched the exchange with growing admiration. For the first time since he'd been put in jail, and then transferred to the psych ward, he felt he had a chance. He might actually taste freedom again.

And it was all on account of Jeremy.

Jeremy Slater was twenty-five years old. He was a big, beefy man with a full beard, short cropped dark hair, and an easy smile. Today he wore his usual jeans, a blue flannel shirt and work boots. He was built like an offensive lineman, a position he'd played on the high school football team. He was fresh out of college having just received his master's degree in counseling from the University of Minnesota. Newly licensed as a mental health professional, working for Bison County was not only his first job, but Ebar was his first client, which is what Jeremy had been told to call the patients by his new boss, Doctor Richard Andrews.

"The idea is to build some distance between you and the client," the doctor had told him after he'd been hired. "I don't want you to get too close to any of them."

It was something that was hard for Jeremy to do. He genuinely liked his first patient, um, client, even though he'd only know him for a day.

After the nurse left, Jeremy pulled up a chair and sat next to the bed. He removed his briefcase from his backpack, opened it and took out the file he'd started the day before. The records from the police indicted the man's name was Kyle Johnson. He was fifty-seven years old and lived in Orchard Lake, a small community thirty miles south of Ryerson, where they were now, the county seat and location of the psychiatric unit of the Bison Country Hospital.

Yesterday, when they'd first met, Jeremy had been struck by how unremarkable his patient looked. That's right, patient, not client. *To heck with what Andrews had said*, Jeremy thought to himself. The people under his care would always be referred to as patients because that's what they were – patients. People who needed help. Help Jeremy hoped he could give them, starting with Kyle.

He smiled. Kyle was smooth shaven, had neatly trimmed sandy hair, brown eyes and wore black framed glasses. He was just under six feet tall and had a thin build. He was about as normal looking as could be, and Jeremy was looking forward to this second meeting to find out more about him. Even though they'd just met for a few minutes the day before, one look today told him his new patient wasn't doing well.

"It says here you're still being medicated. Is that correct?" Jeremy asked, scanning Ebar's chart.

"Yes. At least once a day. It's hard to remember how often because of the drugs. I'm sorry. I wish I could be more specific, but I just can't recall. I'm completely out of it."

The poor guy. Jeremy consulted his notes and then the chart. "They keep track of everything here. You were arrested and put in jail on August 11th. Today's August 16th. You've been here since August 12th. It appears you're being given a shot to relax you three times a day. I'm going to talk to Doctor Franklin." Jeremy picked up his phone and tapped out a quick text to the doctor. "I'll get to the bottom of this."

"Thank you so much," Ebar said, fighting back an unexpected tear. He picked up a Kleenex from the table next to his bed and dabbed at his eyes. "I feel like I'm a prisoner."

Jeremy reached over and touched his patient's arm in a

gesture of solidary. "Well, in a way, you kind of are. But I'll stick with you and do what I can to help - both you and the situation."

Ebar breathed a sigh of relief. *Finally!* "Thank you," he said. He was quiet for a minute and watched while Jeremy consulted his notes. He felt so comfortable with the young mental health worker. So relaxed. He decided to do something he'd always wanted to do, but never had the opportunity. Or never, for that matter, knew anyone he felt he could tell his secret to. Jeremy seemed different, a person he felt he could trust.

Ebar cleared his throat, and Jeremy looked up from his notes.

"Are you okay?" he asked, a concerned looked on his face. "Those drugs can sometimes make you thirsty. Can I get you some water or something?"

Ebar took a deep breath and let it out. Then he smiled. "No, I'm okay. I just…If you don't mind, I have something to tell you."

"Oh, really." Jeremy closed his file and sat back to pay full attention. "What's up?"

"Well, there's no easy way to say this. It's personal. Are you sure you won't tell anyone?"

"I'm positive," Jeremy said, leaning forward. "Look, everything between us is confidential. You can tell me anything." He smiled a warm smile. "I'm on your side, remember?"

"That's good to know, because I've never told this to anyone."

"What is it?"

"Well, you might not believe it, but it's the truth."

Jeremy was beginning to get nervous. *Was this guy going to confess to being serial killed or something? God, then what would he do?* He admonished himself and his overactive imagination. Never mind. He'd cross that bridge when he got to it.

Jeremy shifted in his chair, folded his hands in his lap and looked at his patient with kind eyes. "Just spit it out," he encouraged. "We'll take it from there."

"Okay. Here goes." Ebar looked at Jeremy and saw a person who was waiting patiently, if not a little anxiously. *I'm sure I can trust him*, he thought, and then forged ahead. "What I have to say is this. I'm an alien. My real name is Ebar, and I come from the planet Rykos."

Chapter Three

AFTER EBAR OPENED up with the truth about being an alien, Jeremy immediately took charge and became his advocate. He set up counseling sessions, monitored Ebar's progress, or Kyle, as he was known to the staff at the psych ward as well as to the police and everyone else, and eventually got him transferred to the Ryerson Group Home half a mile from the hospital.

Throughout the next month, the two became close. Ebar appreciated two things about Jeremy. One, that the young mental health counselor didn't think he was crazy like everyone one else, and two, that Jeremy even entertained the notion that Ebar really was the alien he said he was.

Jeremy, for his part, genuinely liked the quiet, mild-mannered, middle-aged man, who's chart said he was fifty-seven, old enough to be his own father, although his neatly trimmed, sandy hair and penetrating green eyes behind his dark framed glasses, made him look twenty years younger.

At the group home, Ebar's room was on the second floor. It was a small ten by ten-foot space in a one-hundred and fifty-year-old Victorian house located just off main street in the town of twenty-five thousand inhabitants.

That morning Ebar been given some free time and was using it to read a favorite book, *Walden*. He was sitting on his narrow bed when he heard a knock on the door frame.

Looking up, he smiled, and set the book aside. "Jeremy. Hi. Good to see you. How's is going?"

"Hi. It's going okay," Jeremy said, his friendly greeting belying the look of concern on his face.

The young counselor swung by every other day or so to check on his patient. Those informal visits were in addition to the state mandated twice a week individual counseling sessions Jeremy conducted. Ebar also attended group sessions led by Doctor Franklin, the same man who'd been prescribing medications for him ever since he'd first been admitted to the psych ward at the hospital a month earlier. The drugs were now different, not as strong, thanks to Jeremy's insistence, but Ebar was still medicated, something that both of them were learning to live with.

"You've got to choose your battles," Jeremy told Ebar once. "Besides, there's not much we can do about it. Doctor

Franklin pretty much rules the roost around here when it comes to prescribing meds for the patients."

Ebar had no argument against that, so he'd said, "Okay. It's fine. You're the boss," kind of making a joke.

At the time, Jeremy grinned, "Well, actually, the guy I report to, Doctor Richard Andrews, is my boss, but I appreciate your confidence in me. Maybe one day."

It was one thing Ebar appreciated about Jeremy - he had a sense of humor and didn't take himself too seriously. Not like a lot of the other doctors and counselors and people he'd been running into lately. It was always good to see him.

"So, to what do I owe this visit?" Ebar asked. "You look a little preoccupied. Here just to chat? Our next session isn't until tomorrow. Is everything okay?"

Jeremy grimaced and fidgeted with a strap on his backpack. "Well, speaking of bosses, it's actually not going all that good. I just came from a meeting with my boss - that Andrews guy I've told you about."

"How'd it go?" Ebar asked. He was all ears. When Jeremy first arrived, he'd hoped his counselor was bringing some good news for a change, like, for instance, when he might be released. But a closer look at Jeremy's concerned expression told him something was wrong. In a big way. Ebar felt his stomach flip over. "Oh, oh. What'd he say?" He suddenly felt sick. Nauseous. "Your boss. He said something bad about me. I just know it."

"Kind of, I'm afraid." Jeremy nervously set his backpack aside and turned to Ebar with a pained look. "Look. I'll give you a recap. You need to hear this. It's not all good news."

13

Ebar sat up, ready to pay attention. He trusted his counselor to do what was right for him. "Fire away. I'm ready for anything."

Jeremy pulled up a chair from Ebar's desk and sat down. "Okay. I'll give you the highlights."

The world of social work was not the utopian dream job of helping people that Jeremy imagined it was going to be, a bitter truth he'd found out earlier that day.

That morning had been the monthly Wednesday meeting at the Bison County Government Center, a time when Jeremy and the three other mental health professionals updated their supervisor, Doctor Richard Andrews, the state assigned psychiatrist who oversaw their work, on the progress they were making with their clients. Having only been hired for just over one month, it had been the first time Jeremy had attended the meeting. He was last to give his update.

"So, Mr. Slater, welcome to your first meeting," Doctor Andrews had said, turning to face his young employee. Andrews was a man whose immense ego barely fit in the cramped conference room. He looked at Jeremy from behind tortoise shell designer eyeglasses as benevolently benevolent as he imagined himself to be. "Tell us, how are things going with your alien? He got into that fight at the sewage treatment plant, right?"

After speaking the words, 'your alien' two of the other case workers, Steven Wallace and Soren Kucinen had laughed on cue. It was something Jeremy was beginning to expect whenever his case was talked about. What he didn't expect was that Julie Brooks had joined them in their laughter. She was the lone female in the group and had become not only a friend but a mentor of sorts over the past month. At least she had glanced in his direction, made eye contact, and had shrugged, offering him a chagrined smile.

Sorry, she'd mouthed silently.

Slightly rattled, Jeremy had taken a sip of water to give himself a moment and get his thoughts in order. Then he'd answered the question. "He's doing fine, doctor. Just fine."

"Really?" Andrews had questioned, leaning forward in a slightly threatening manner and steepling his fingers. "From where I sit, that's not the case at all." He starred at Jeremy. "Let's review the facts, shall we?" His condescending attitude grated on Jeremy's nerves, but he kept his emotions in check. Andrews held up his hand and began counting off using his fingers. "One, he got into that fight at the sewage plant and nearly killed a guy. Two, he was put in jail and started going on and on about being an alien and needing to make his transmissions or whatever to some guy on a planet in some faraway galaxy. Three, he got moved to the psych ward for evaluation." Here, Andrews paused, pointed a finger, and said, "An evaluation of a guy who has obvious problems, paid for by the state and conducted by you. And four, you have the nerve to sit there and tell me he's doing just fine." Andrews had sat back and shaken his head sadly at what Jeremy could only surmise was his nativity, and said, "I don't think so. It doesn't sound like he's doing fine at all." Andrews paused for a moment before leaning forward and commanding, "Explain yourself."

Jeremy had wiped a bead of sweat from his forehead. After the dressing down from his boss, he couldn't shake the feeling that he was being set-up. But he didn't care. He had genuine feelings for his first patient, known to most people familiar with the case as *The Alien of Orchard Lake*, and he felt he owed it to Ebar to tell his side of the story.

"Okay," Jeremy had said, nervously clearing his throat as he accepted the challenge. "Where do you want me to begin?"

Andrews had sat back in his chair, taken a sip of herbal tea, and made it a point of glancing at his wristwatch, an expensive looking Rolex. "Wherever you want. You've got ten minutes."

Better than nothing. "Okay, here goes." Jeremy had looked around the room, making eye contact with everyone as he'd begun speaking. "You all know his back story, right?" Around the table both Wallace and Kucinen nodded. Julie did, too, but she also had given him the thumbs up sign for good luck. Seeing it, Jeremy had smiled to himself, thinking, *at least she's on my side.*

He'd continued, "Okay, you know his earth name is Kyle Johnson, right? But his real name is Ebar, which is what I'm going to call him. He says he's been on earth for just over fifty years. He was sent by Zenon, the ruler of the planet Rykos which is located in the galaxy Foorm." At that point, Jeremy had stopped talking and looked around the room. All eyes were on him. *At least I have their attention,* he had thought to himself, although he wished Andrews would wipe that disconcerting smirk off his face.

"Ruler Zenon wanted to explore deep into space. I guess he liked to take over planets or something. From what Ebar has told me, the guy isn't very nice and kind of an egotistical tyrant. Ebar, by the way, volunteered for the mission. He told me that he did it because he didn't have

16

much else going on in his life."

Julie had laughed out loud at that statement and been immediately admonished by a stern look from Andrews. Jeremy could have hugged her. At least the outburst had broken the tension in the room. A little bit, anyway.

He continued. "Zenon had chosen earth because of all its water. That's what Ebar told me. Apparently, it's in short support on their planet. Zenon thought if earth was worth taking over, we would all be killed and be replaced with citizens of Rykos. Ebar was sent through a space-time portal and ended up in San Francisco in 1967. You know, the Summer of Love? I guess it sort of freaked him out."

At that point, Steve Wallace had spoken up. "What'd he look like, anyway, when he arrived back then, this alien of yours? I have an image of something like that 'ET' character in the movie. You'd have thought someone would have noticed."

"Well, that's just it. He immediately Shape Changed into a human form dressed like the people around him."

"So…like a hippy?"

"Yeah, I guess."

Wallace shook his head. "Weird."

"In fact, he's Shape Changed a lot since he's been on earth. It's helped him fit in. Plus, he can change his age, too. All in all, he's a pretty remarkable guy."

At that point, Jeremy had paused and looked around the round the room, expecting questions. But there had been none, only a trio of skeptical gazes from Andrews, Wallace and Kucinen. Not Julie, however. She had smiled at him and given him another surreptitious thumbs up sign.

"Okay, moving on," he'd continued. "Ebar eventually made his way to Minnesota. He settled in the little town of Orchard Lake, just south of here, and..."

"We all know where Orchard Lake is, Slater," Andrews had interjected, looking at his Rolex. He was obviously nearing the end of his patience, which, on a good day wasn't much, and what he was hearing from Jeremy right now wasn't making this day one of his better ones. "Time's about up. So, tell us, what did this alien of yours do when he got to Minnesota? Join a freak show? Or a commune?"

Steve Wallace and Soren Kucinen had both laughed, and Andrews graced their reaction with a nod and a smile. Jeremy felt a trickle of sweat run down his back. This wasn't going too well. But Julie had taken that moment to give him an encouraging smile, which Jeremy appreciated. Then she had made an imperceptible motion for him to continue, which he had done. He'd also been relived to find she was still on his side.

"Well, no, sir," Jeremy had told Andrews, regaining some of his confidence. "He didn't do any of those things. He just started living."

Before Andrews could say anything derogative, Julie had leaned forward and said, "Interesting. Tell us about that."

Jeremey had smiled at her and said, "Well, he tried to fit into the community. Most of you know Orchard Lake. It's not huge, only about eight thousand people. Ebar rented an apartment. Did various jobs. Got to know people. And, more importantly for him and his mission, he sent back

18

regular reports to Zenon. He called them communiques. They were about life in the United States, specifically around Orchard Lake. He worked many years at the local hardware store before landing the job at the sewage treatment facility. He'd only worked there for three or four months before..." Here Jeremy had paused before continuing. "Before the altercation."

At that point, he had quit talking and looked around the room. He'd been pleased to see he still had their attention, and that all eyes were focused on him. "You've heard about that incident with one of the other employees, right? Ebar got in that fight, ended up in jail, and then was transferred to the psych ward in the hospital. That's where he was when I was given his case. Now he's in the group home here in town." He held up his hand. "And that's about it." He stopped talking, then had thought to ask, "Oh, are there any questions?"

"So, end of story?" Soren Kucinen had asked. Normally quiet as a mouse, Jeremy had been pleased to see he had Kucinen's interest.

"Not really," Jeremy had said.

"What? Sounds like it to me. Why not?" Kucinen had looked puzzled and was about to say something else when Andrews cut him off.

"Exactly," he'd interjected. "That's exactly what I was thinking. Why? What happened?"

Jeremy had been glad to see that even Doctor Andrews was now interested.

"Well, after years and years of sending back his communiques to Commander Zenon on regular basis, something strange happened. A few months ago, a few weeks before the time of the fight, Ebar suddenly got no response in return from Zenon. He tried and tried, but it was like Zenon and Rykos had completely vanished from the universe."

"Nothing?" Julie had asked. "He didn't hear anything from them?"

"Nope. Nothing."

"Wow," she'd said.

The room had gone silent. Jeremy had had the sudden thought that they were thinking about what they would do if they were in a situation similar to Ebar's. Maybe they were even thinking how frightening it would be to suddenly have lost all contact with your home planet and be stranded in the middle of the universe like Ebar had been. It had to have been an incredibly lonely feeling.

Then Jeremy had mentally slapped himself. What was he thinking? The chance of anything remotely sympathetic toward Ebar coming out of this group was a big fat zero. Even he sometimes had trouble believing that his patient really was an alien, a fact that he didn't bother mentioning to anyone, not even Julie. Or Ebar, for that matter.

Jeremy had continued, "I think Ebar had a mental breakdown at the sewage treatment plant as a result of having lost communication with his home planet. His fear of being abandoned and stranded alone was overwhelming. Knowing he was left with no way of getting in touch with anyone was just too much. I think those two factors had something to do with him getting into that fight. He just snapped and lashed out. So, with that in mind..." Jeremy had hurried along before anyone (like Andrews) could contradict him, "With that in mind, I want to do is this: I want to help my client integrate back into our world. Imagine what he must be going through. For nearly fifty years he's been able to communicate with Zenon and Rykos but now he can't. He's devasted and, I think, acted out on those feelings of fear and loneliness by getting into that altercation. I think I can help him."

"How?" Andrews had asked with a challenging tone in his voice. "He sounds like a freak if you ask me."

"Oh, no, doctor. He's not. He's very real and has very real emotions. Almost human."

Andrews had smirked. "I'll bet."

"I'll show you," Jeremy had told him, starting to get angry. "I'll show you those communiques of his. He's kept every single one of them for all these years, and he's shared them with me. They're quite remarkable and show a sensitivity to people on earth, and in the Orchard Lake community specifically, that is really quite remarkable. They'll show you that he's worth trying to help."

Doctor Andrews had smirked, sat back, and looked for a long minute at the young mental health worker. Then he'd sat forward, folded his hands on the table and said, "I doubt it. I really do, but I'll admit, I'm intrigued. A man who's convinced he's an alien? To me, it's not only a waste of time, but money as well. They should just send him back to jail, try him for assault and let the chips fall where they may."

Jeremy's sinking feeling in his stomach upon hearing those words was immediately replaced when Andrews had waved a hand as if batting away a fly and added, "But it's the county's dime that's paying for all of this, so go ahead and knock yourself out, Slater. Show me." He looked around the room and added, "In fact, show us all. We'll have a special meeting next week. Wednesday, a week from today. Bring one of those communiques or transmissions or whatever to show us, and we'll take it from there."

Jeremy's heart raced. What a break! "Thank you, sir," Jeremy had told his boss, but had received only a glassy glare in return. Andrew's steely eyes pierced his own like lasers. It was right then that a light had switched on in Jeremy's brain, and he had realized Andrews didn't like him very much. If at all. But that was okay. There was a bigger issue here, and it had to do with how people who had mental issues were treated. Jeremy liked Ebar, and he was excited to do the best he could to help his patient get better.

The meeting had broken up shortly thereafter. Jeremy had put his papers in his briefcase and slid the briefcase into his backpack. He'd been painfully aware that Wallace and Kucinen had studiously avoided him and hurried out of the meeting room together. Andrews had taken out his phone and was soon engaged in a heated conversation about something Jeremy couldn't make out. Standing by himself, he had nervously run his fingers through his beard, feeling like the world's biggest outsider.

Sensing his discomfort, Julie had come up to him. She was a petite woman in her late thirties with short cropped blond hair, large brown eyes serious expression that couldn't always hide her wicked sense of humor. She was about a foot shorter and seventy-five pounds lighter than

Jeremy, and he appreciated it when she asked, "How are you doing?"

"Oh, fine. I guess." He indicated with his head that he didn't want to talk in front of Andrews.

"Want to go for coffee?" She'd asked.

"Sure," Jeremy had said, still slightly distracted by the meeting.

"How about the café down the street?"

"The Mainstreet Diner? That'd be fine."

"Want to walk?"

Jeremy had glanced at Andrews who was now talking animatedly. He turned to Julie, "Yeah, I do. Plus, to be perfectly honest, after dealing with Andrews, I could use some fresh air."

***

Jeremy and Julie walked out of the building and headed for the café a block away. Behind them Doctor Andrews stayed on the phone for a long time. He was talking to an acquaintance he knew in the Department of Defense. They'd met in college and remained close friends, both having a burning desire to make names for themselves in their chosen professions.

"Let me tell you, Phil, this could be big. Really big."

Phil was Phil Jorgenson, an assistant in the office of information for NASA, the National Aeronautics and Space Administration.

"I hear you, Rich," Jorgenson had responded. "But an alien? Really, that's a little far-fetched."

"I know it sounds crazy, and, truthfully, it might be nothing."

"No kidding."

"But, then again, if it's true, man, can you imagine? I'd be famous."

"Or, made out to be a complete fool. Don't forget Worchoski a few years back."

Both of them paused, thinking about the eminent astrophysicist at a prestigious eastern college who for a time had been convinced he was communicating with another galaxy. It turned out he was only chatting online with some hackers from east Asia.

Andrews spoke up. "Yeah, I know. But what if Slater is right? What if this guy really is an alien?"

"Well, then, my friend, you would be famous."

"You would be, too."

"How do you figure?"

"The way I figure it, I'll handle the psychological aspects of the guy, and you can handle the space stuff. I have no clue about any of that."

"Hmm." Phil went quiet for a moment, thinking. *If Andrews is right, and if the guy really is an alien, this could be the biggest thing to hit since... Since...Well, it'd the biggest thing ever!* "You know what?" he finally said. "I like your thinking, my friend."

Andrews smiled. "I thought you would."

"Keep me posted, okay."

"Oh, yeah. I will."

"You and that Slater fella and the rest are meeting next week?"

"Yeah."

"Call me when you're done."

"Oh, yeah. You bet I will."

After they disconnected, Andrew stood up and walked to the window and looked out. Down the block he thought he saw Julie and Jeremy walking together but couldn't be sure. He turned to the conference table, picked up his papers and left the room, thinking that next week's meeting could be the start of something big for him. Just think. My own alien. He grinned. Or, how about this? "Andrew's Alien", he said out loud. Then he smiled a big smile. He liked the sound of that. He liked it a lot.

Chapter Four

EBAR HAD LISTENED carefully to Jeremy's recap of the meeting, intrigued by the young counselor going to bat for him. He was also touched and still getting used to the reality having an advocate on his side.

"So, it sounds like Andrews wasn't too excited about what you told him about me."

"It's complicated. I think he likes to think you might be an alien, but he's letting his rational mind get in the way."

"Seems like it," Ebar said, thoughtfully. He took off his

glasses and polished them with a handkerchief before putting them back on. "Sounds like your friend Julie is different, though. How'd coffee go?"

Jeremy smiled. "It went well. We had a nice, long talk. You want to hear about it?"

Ebar fluffed up his pillow and sat back against wall. "Absolutely. Fire away!" On his nightstand was a lamp, a clock, and a bottle of water. He opened the water and had a sip. Ever polite, he indicated the bottle and said, "I wish I had one for you, but I'm allowed only one bottle at a time. They monitor us pretty closely here." He looked toward the door, or where the door would have been. Rules were that the patients couldn't close themselves off from the rest of the population. They could have their privacy, such as it was, but no closed doors. There were no doors on any of the patients' rooms at the group home. They'd all been removed years ago.

"That's okay," Jeremy said. "I've got one right here." He opened his backpack and took out a bottle, unscrewed the cap and drank.

"So, about Julie? What'd you guys talk about?"

"Well, first off, she told me about the trip she and her partner Wren are taking."

"Where are they going?"

"They've got an RV and are going on a vacation to Yellowstone Park. You know, out in Wyoming? They'll be gone a couple of weeks."

A wistful look came over Ebar. "A vacation? I've never been on one before. It sounds like fun. When are they leaving?"

"We've got the big meeting next Wednesday, a week from today, and they're leaving that next Friday."

"You know I've always…"

Jeremy cut him off. "Geez, Ebar. We didn't talk hardly at all about their vacation."

"Oh."

"You've got to understand that what's going on with you is a very big deal," Jeremy said, heatedly. "It's serious. So that's what we talked about. We talked about you."

"Me? Really?"

"Yes. It had to do with my plan to help you. You remember what I told them at the meeting? About your communiques?"

Ebar leaned forward. "Yeah?"

"Well, Julie wondered what the communiques were about."

"You told her?"

"Well, generally, I did. I know we have patient privilege, but I felt it was the right thing to do."

"I don't mind. Anything to help get me out of here."

"That's good."

"So, what did you tell her about them?"

"I told her that I'd only skimmed through them and hadn't really read any of them very thoroughly."

Ebar grinned. "There's a lot there."

"Yeah, there is. I mentioned the ones I remembered. You know, about the squirrel hunter and the hole in the ice.

Those stood out"

"What'd she'd think?"

"She said that she thought they sounded interesting."

Ebar took a drink of water. "Well, that's something, I guess."

"Let me explain." Jeremy took out Ebar's file, which after a month of sessions was nearly an inch thick. He also took out his phone and his laptop.

"My, goodness." Ebar joked nervously. "Should I be worried?"

"I don't think so. Julie and I started to rough out a plan for next week's meeting."

"Okay…"

"Remember I told Andrews and Wallace and Kucinen that I was going to share your communiques with them?"

"Yes. And you still think that's a good idea?"

"Well, I did at the time, but, honestly, I'm not sure I was thinking too clearly. I was kind of rattled by Andrews."

"He's kind of a jerk."

"Yeah, he is. But he's also in charge, and I wanted to stay working with you, so I said the first thing that came into my mind. I didn't really think it through."

"So, Julie helped get your thinking straight?"

"She did."

"What'd she suggest?"

"She thought I should summarize your communiques and let Andrews and Wallace and Kucinen see your 'human side,'" Jeremy said, using finger quotes.

"My human side?"

"Yes, she thought it was best to show them that you're really a human being who's confused and only 'thinks' he's an alien." Finger quotes again.

"But I'm not a human. I'm an alien."

"That's what I told her."

"What'd she say to that?"

"She said that then we might have a problem."

"Oh."

"Yeah. She said that I needed to make a decision."

"A decision?"

"Yes."

"About what?"

"About you."

"Me? How so?"

"Well..."

Jeremy sighed and looked at Ebar who was staring at him, fully engaged, eyes wide open. Ebar's nervousness was palatable. Even his hands were shaking. "It's not good, is it?"

Ignoring the question, Jeremy said, "She told me that I have to decide whether or not I believe you are an alien. 'You're riding the fence with your patient,' is what she said to me. 'You can't have it both ways. Either you're dealing with Kyle, a confused individual who needs your help. Or you're dealing with Ebar, a true to life alien from another planet in another galaxy. In which case you've got a whole different set of issues to deal with.'"

"Wow," Ebar said. "She didn't pull any punches, did she?"

"No, she didn't," Jeremy responded. "And she's right. I do have to make a decision. About you."

The two of them were quiet for a minute, both thinking. Finally, Ebar got up and went to his dresser and took out a box of papers. He held them in his hands and fought back tears that suddenly formed. Jeremy could see they were the communiques, the only connection Ebar now had with his home planet. Although many people had seen them, specifically the police and doctor Franklin, the only person who really had taken the time to read any of them had been Jeremy. It was reading some of the communiques that had convinced him that there was a degree of truth in what Ebar was saying. That he really could be an alien.

Jeremy's heart suddenly went out to his patient. "Here, Ebar. Let me have a look at those."

"Why? What good can they do if no one believes me?"

Jeremy took a deep breath and made a fateful decision, one that would change his life forever. Julie was right. He had been riding the fence, and he couldn't have it both ways. It was time to decide. "Okay, let me tell you this, Ebar. I believe you." He stood up and went to his patient and looked him square in the eyes. "I believe you. I really do. I believe you are an alien."

Ebar felt weak in his knees. Jeremy caught him by the elbow and guided him to the chair at the desk by the window. Ebar sat down and looked gratefully at his counselor. "You really believe me?"

Jeremy fought an urge to 'cross his heart' like he and his friends used to do when they were kids. Instead, he looked Ebar with as sincere an expression as he could muster and said, "Yes, I do, Ebar. I believe you. I promise."

Ebar gave a sigh of relief and smiled. "You're sure?"

"I am."

A wide smile broke out on Ebar's face, but it quickly faded. "But do you think you can help me? Really and truly? That big meeting's coming up next week. That's pretty fast."

Jeremy wasn't sure at all because he had no idea what he was going to do. But that's not what he told Ebar. Instead, what he said was, "Yes. I very sure." He took the stack of communiques and started spreading them out on the bed. "Let's take a look at what we've got here."

Jeremey's mind was racing because there was something else he and Julie had talked about; something that was now painfully clear the more he thought about it. If Ebar was an alien, what exactly did Jeremy hope to accomplish by helping him? Integrate him back into civilian life so he could return to work as a sewage treatment employee? That seemed a little far-fetched. Once word of Ebar being an alien leaked out, the news media would go crazy for the story. Jeremy could just see it - the press would have a field day. Ebar's picture would be plastered all over not only newspapers and cable news shows, but social media as well. His life would change forever, and probably not for the best.

Ebar didn't need that. What he needed was to somehow

establish communication with commander Zenon and his home planet Rykos. That's what would make him feel better and restore his mental health. But Jeremy's boss, doctor Andrews, and the others like Wallace and Kucinen wouldn't go for that. After all, treat some guy who believes one-hundred percent that he's an alien? No way. That's what they'd be thinking. In fact, they'd probably think Jeremy was nuts himself. Andrews might even fire him, and maybe, just maybe, have him committed. He and Ebar could end up being patients together.

Enough! Jeremy shook his head to clear the garbage thoughts from his mind. Talk about a conundrum. He'd have to tread very carefully. And he'd have to make sure Ebar understood the issues they faced. If Ebar wanted people to accept him, they'd have to accept him as Kyle the sewage treatment employee, not Ebar, the refugee alien from another galaxy.

Jeremy looked at his patient. Against all the advice he'd ever heard from people who'd been in the mental health business a lot longer than him, and against everything he'd learned in college and training to be a mental health professional, Jeremy was slowly coming to two honest conclusions: One, yes, he did think Ebar was telling the truth, and that he really was an alien, a real live, honest to goodness alien, and that he, Jeremy, was his counselor. And two, it was dawning him - against all logic - that Ebar was more than just a patient. He was becoming his friend. Something he'd never expected in his wildest dreams.

We'll cross that bridge when we get to it, Jeremey thought to himself. Which might be the at the meeting next Wednesday. There was a lot riding on it. And Jeremy still didn't know exactly what exactly he was going to do.

But he did know one thing. "I have an idea," he said to Ebar.

"What's that?"

"Let's talk about what happened at the sewage treatment plant and see if we can figure something out."

Ebar smiled and went right to his box of communiques. "I can help you."

"How so."

"Before the fight, I had written a couple of communiques to commander Zenon." He started flipping through pages until he found what he was looking for. "No one has seen them yet. Not even you. I was kind of saving them, but I have no idea why." He took out a paper-clipped bunch of papers and handed them to Jeremy. "Here you go. Like with all my other communiques, I wrote these out, so I'd have an idea of what to say when I got in touch with Zenon."

Jeremy took the papers and held them in his lap. He looked at Ebar. "Say, now that we're talking about it, I was wondering...how's that work, anyway? Getting in touch with your commander?"

Ebar grinned at what Jeremy could only surmise as pleasant memories, and said, "I connect telepathically with him. Then I read what I wrote to myself, and the message goes out to Zenon all the way to Rykos. Like high energy brain waves." He smiled at Jeremy. "Pretty slick, isn't it?"

Jeremy had no idea what Ebar was talking about, but he did know one thing, having the ability to connect with another person in another galaxy was, indeed, pretty slick.

"It is," he said, and took the communique Ebar handed him. It was about twenty pages long. Handwritten. Jeremy paged through them. "I guess I've got some reading to do." Then he checked his watch. "Oh, wow. Geez, I'm sorry. I've got another meeting to get to."

"That's okay. Maybe we can talk tomorrow. It's Thursday, our regular session," Ebar said.

"Good idea." Jeremy indicated the papers. "I'll have reviewed these by then."

"Great."

Jeremy stuffed the pages in his briefcase and put them and his laptop in his backpack. "Okay, I'm going to get going. I'll see you tomorrow. You remember the time?"

"Yep. Ten in the morning. The downstair meeting room."

"Okay." Jeremy picked up his phone and got to his feet. "Good. Okay, I'll see you then."

They shook hands.

Ebar waved goodbye as Jeremy left the room. He hadn't felt this good in months. Now, if only he could just get out of the group home, that'd be great. He hadn't been entirely truthful with the young counselor, who Ebar could tell was becoming attached to him. Well, that was good. That would work to his advantage. After all, he'd need help if he was to ever to get back to Rykos. Because that's what he needed to do. He needed to re-establish communication with commander Zenon and tell them to come and get him. That incident at the sewage treatment plant had been too close of a call. He'd lost his temper, something that had never

36

happened before. It was time to go home. It was time to leave earth, and he needed to get in touch with Zenon to work out a plan. If not, he was stuck here forever.

Chapter Five

THE NEXT MORNING at ten o'clock, Jeremy came in the front entrance of the Ryerson Group Home. He greeted Clara Simpson, the house manager, and said "Hi" to a few of the orderlies on his way to where the meeting room was located. The group home held seventeen patients and was nearly always full. It had a positive reputation in the mental healthcare community, and Jeremy was glad he had been able to place Ebar there.

He entered the room, a small space in the back of the building. A window overlooked an alley, and the back entrances to a number of one and story business on the street behind. The room was austere, only a print of the north shore of Lake Superior on one wall, and a round table in the middle of the room with six metal folding chairs scattered around it. Jeremy sat down facing the door and took out his phone and laptop and Ebar's file.

He also took out the water treatment communique and laid it on the table. Wow, he thought to himself, and not for the first time since he'd read the remarkable story. What Ebar had done at the sewage treatment plant was pretty amazing as far as he was concerned. And not just the fight, either, but the work he performed there as well. It was pretty impressive as far as he was concerned.

Just then Ebar popped his head around the corner of the door frame. "Anyone home?" he joked.

Jeremy cracked a smile. "Come on in."

Ebar sat down next to him and took a drink from his ever-present bottle of water. "How's it going?" He pointed at the communique. "Did you get a chance to read it?"

"I sure did. It's pretty remarkable."

Ebar's face turned red with a flush. "How do you mean?"

"Well, all things considered, and I'm no lawyer or anything, but I don't think what you did was all that wrong."

"Well, I did beat the guy up."

"I know, but he had it coming to him."

"I appreciate that, but he pressed charges, so the cops were obligated to hold me. In fact, they picked me up at work the next day. Now there's this…" he waved his hand, taking in the room. "Now I'm locked up here, and people think I'm nuts."

Jeremy responded with what he hoped was an encouraging smile. "Well, I don't."

"Thank you. I appreciate it, but what are we going to do?"

"I think we can use this communique to our advantage."

"Really?"

"Yes, I do."

Jeremy sat back with the papers in his hand. "Let's do this. I've reviewed what you wrote a few times. My thought is that I should read it to the group next week at the meeting. I think your communique speaks for itself, and it will give Andrews and the others a flavor for what you are all about. How's that sound?"

Ebar didn't hesitate. "If you think it's a good idea, I'll go along with it. Anything to speed the process along. I'd love to get out of here and go on living my life."

"And I want to help," Jeremy said.

"Great." Ebar took a drink of water. "What's your plan?"

Jeremy shuffled through the papers. "How about if I read it out loud right now? We can see how it sounds, and if we need to add or delete anything. What do you think?"

"Kind of like a practice run?"

Jeremy nodded, "Yeah, like that."

Ebar was relieved that they were making some progress. "Okay. Great. Go ahead. You're the boss."

41

Jeremy smiled. "I don't know about that, but let's give it a shot."

"I'm all for it," Ebar said. "Fire away."

Jeremy cleared his throat, took a sip of water, and glanced at Ebar, who watched him expectantly. Then he began reading the communique out loud, just like it had been written:

"Communique from Ebar on planet earth

Subject: The Water Treatment Plant

To: Commander Zenon on the planet Rykos

Man, just a little peace and quiet, please. I was trying to concentrate on titrating a sample solution to determine whether it was acidic or basic, and I needed to keep my hand steady. My lab was across the building's common area from my boss's office, Lou Henderson, but the two men's voices coming from inside were loud and angry and could easily be heard through the closed door. They were arguing again.

"Damn it all anyway, Al, I told you not to bring it up anymore." Lou was trying to make his point, and by the sound of his voice, I could tell he was quickly losing patience.

"Look," Al said. "I can make good money. Double time on Sundays. Triple time on holidays."

"But only if I okay the extra hours, and I'm not going to do that. So, get your act together and haul your ass back to work."

"Look, Lou, just give me a chance to make a little extra cash. I need it for Johnny. He's starting college in two months."

"Out!" I heard Lou yell and could easily visualize him pointing toward the door. "Get outta' here right now."

The door slammed open, and Al stormed out. "Screw you, Lou," he muttered under his breath.

Al stomped through the common area and pushed through the glass door leading outside. I heard his truck start up and its engine revving. Then, after a moment, it tore off, tires spinning and gravel flying, pinging off the door.

Geez, I thought to myself, turning back to continue the titration. I didn't like conflict and was a little upset at the outburst. My hand shook slightly. *What a hell of a place to work.*

Orchard Lake is a relatively small town of eight-thousand located in eastern Bison County. I'm part of the Public Works Department and my job is to test the water quality of the city's sewage treatment plant. It's mid-May and I've only been working here for about a month and never really had any problems or issues. Except for Al. He's kind of a jerk.

My boss, Lou, is a no-nonsense man around thirty-five who runs public works with an iron fist. He's a short, stocky, muscular guy, who likes to hunt and fish whenever he can. But he's also one-hundred percent committed to the Orchard Lake community and doing the best job he can for them. His background in the military probably accounted for some of that. Like he's told me more than once, "First and foremost the military taught me discipline, Kyle. I learned to depend on myself, but also to depend on my team. It's how we got things done over there."

Over there was Afghanistan, where Lou had ended up as a marine Sergeant leading his squad on search and destroy missions in the hills in and around Kunar Province. He's been back for ten years now and has been enjoying a relatively peaceful life with a job over-seeing what is basically the maintenance of the entire Orchard Lake community. The water treatment department where I work is just one of the departments that Lou oversees, but it's an important one.

Just prior to me being hired, the city had been put on notice by the Metropolitan Waste Commission (MWC). The city of Orchard Lake was in jeopardy of being sued because of its poor water testing procedures. I had been hired to clean up the city's act, so to speak. "No pun intended," Lou had said to me at the time I was hired. But it wasn't a laughing matter, and Lou had a grim look on his face when he said it, because his job was on the line. He was depending on me to make sure the tests were accurate and within the standards set by the Minnesota Pollution Control Agency (MPCA). So, I had a lot riding on me, which was one thing, but, more importantly, I wanted to do a good job.

I've always loved water. I think that's probably why I volunteered for this mission to earth. I recall once when I was about five, my mom took me to the big reservoir near Kamias. We sat on the edge, our feet dangling in the water and watched the sun set. The evening was peaceful and calm and over the next half hour the sky changed colors from orange to mauve to violet and purple as it sank below the horizon across from us.

"Isn't it beautiful?" I remember mom saying, as she

inhaled the sweet scent of summer in the air.

I leaned up against her and said, "It's the most beautiful sight I've ever seen."

And I meant it. Ever since I was a young kid, there has been something about water and being near it. It was almost a spiritual thing, although I know we aren't supposed to say those kinds of things, but to me it was. I was drawn to water at an early age and still am.

As you know, Commander, over the years I've being working at a number of jobs in the Orchard Lake community. The most recent was at the hardware store stocking shelves and running the cash register. I was unpacking furnace air filters when I overheard a couple of guys talking about the job opening up in the public works department, specifically doing water quality testing. I knew it was the job for me because I'd be helping take care of the city's water supply. I was able to purchase the *Water Quality Standards Handbook* for conducting tests from the Environmental Protection Agency online, so I was all set. I used the handbook and other online resources and easily came up to speed with the tests and how to conduct them. I applied for the job and was granted an interview.

I remember it well. It was the middle of April and the snow had finally melted after a long, cold winter. Lou wore his long-sleeved tan work shirt rolled up tight above his elbows. He put both his arms on his desk, folded his hands and stared straight at me. "Here's the situation, Kyle. Earlier this year the Minnesota Pollution Control Agency sampled our water, you know, the water we send back to the community after it goes through the treatment process. The quality was within the guidelines set by them, but just barely. Then the Metropolitan Waste Commission got involved and threatened to sue us." He shook his head and glanced out the window. I followed his gaze. A man in a pickup truck was pulling into the gravel parking lot. Lou frowned and pointed to the truck before continuing. "That guy out there used to do the tests for us. His name is Al. He's kind of a..." Lou's voice trailed off. The room was quiet until the sound of a bobcat starting up drifted into the window along with a blast of noxious exhaust. "Damn..." Lou got up, closed the window, and then sat back down. "Anyway, his testing methods weren't the best. In his defense, he really wasn't hired to work in the lab, he just volunteered for the extra pay, and we let him. But now we've got the MPCA and the MWC breathing down our necks, not to mention our own city council." He paused again and tapped a finger on his desk, making sure he had my attention. Which he did. "In a nutshell, I need someone to get this lab in order and to get the tests run right so I can get those two agencies off my back." He sat back and gave me a challenging look. "Think you can do it?"

I had all I could do to keep from jumping to my feet, standing at attention, and snapping off a salute. Instead, I said, simply, "Yes, sir. I can do it. You can count on me."

And that was that. I was hired right off the bat. I didn't even have to show any qualifications. Some people might think I was lucky. Maybe. But I think it was meant to be. I started work that following week, after I'd given notice at the hardware store.

That first day, I washing some beakers in the sink when Lou stopped in. "You getting all settled?"

"Sure," I told him. I looked around. My lab space was a

rather cramped area eight feet by twelve feet. No problem. I had adequate counter space and a big sink, plus lots of cupboards, shelves, and drawers for storing glassware and testing equipment. The place had been a mess, though, and I'd spent the morning just cleaning and straightening everything up. I felt good about how things looked, now, though, and said to Lou, "Yeah, I'm doing good. Just making sure everything is organized and clean."

Lou looked around. "Looks better than it's ever looked."

I was pleased. I was learning that my boss was a no non-sense kind of guy, and I wanted him to like me. From that day on, I just focused on running my tests and doing my job. Lou was happy with me, I could tell. He didn't say much, but he'd occasionally stop by to see what I was doing, or to comment and say, "The place never looked better." It was good enough for me.

A few minutes after Al stormed out of his office, Lou followed behind. He was in a hurry and cursing to himself. He hurried by the door to my lab and yelled to me, "I'm out of here for a while."

Once outside, he got into his black Chevy three-quarter ton and sped down the driveway, through the gates and out onto the county road that ran past the twenty-acre area that housed public works and some other buildings. I figured Lou was just mad and needed to blow off some steam and didn't think anything more about it. I still had a full day ahead of me. I finished the titration, wrote up a report, and then checked the calendar on the wall and my watch. It was 1:00 pm on Tuesday. Time to collect some water samples.

A hundred yards from where my lab was located was the water works building where the final processing of the wastewater into potable drinkable water took place. That's where I headed, grabbing a sterilized bottle on the way out the door. It was a perfect spring day in mid-May. I estimated the temperature to be in the high seventies, the humidity was low, and it felt great to be outside. The sky was blue and only a few big, white, puffy clouds were drifting by on a light breeze from the south. I heard a familiar sound and looked around before I finally saw them coming into land, a flock of about two dozen herring gulls that frequented the area, scouring the ground and looking for free handouts.

Herring gulls were a species that were very aggressive, but I liked to see them anyway. They'd often squabble and fight among themselves, but just as often soared on the wind dipping and gliding almost like they were playing. The gulls reminded me watching the yookies at the reservoir back on Rykos with my mom, because they looked kind of like the gulls I was watching now. Only these were not as big. Those yookies, boy, sometimes they grew to the size of a large man, which was pretty amazing, and... Sorry, I digress. The point is that seeing the gulls always brought back pleasant memories of home.

I opened the door and went into the water works building and was immediately struck by how cool the air felt. The final clarification of the treated water took place here. The building was made of cinder blocks and was approximately twenty feet by thirty feet in size. The water was held in the large tank in the center, and it was crystal clear. I could see all the way to the bottom, twelve feet down. The treatment process I'd put into place when I was first hired was working perfectly. The water looked so inviting I had to fight the urge to drive right in, especially on a warm day like today. I bent down and carefully filled the sampling bottle with some of the water and then stood up.

"What you up to, pal?"

"Geez!" I jumped and almost dropped my container. Turning quickly, I saw it was Al moving toward me from behind the shadow of the door. I'd seen him leave earlier after his confrontation with Lou, but never saw him come back. He was sneaky that way. I felt myself instinctively tense up, my muscles contracting. "Man, you scared me."

Al laughed. "Worried about something?"

I'd been working at the facility for a month. The entire time I'd been at my job, my interactions with the other employees had run the gamut from friendly to indifferent. All except for Al. He was the only one who was openly hostile. I figured it had to do with me taking over his former responsibilities doing the water tests.

I tried to shrug it off. "No worries, man. Everything is cool." I didn't know why I talked that way just then, but for some reason I did. Probably because he made me nervous. Along with his bad attitude, he was taller than me by three or four inches and outweighed me by at least fifty pounds.

Lou had warned me about Al early on. "Watch out for him," Lou had said, during a conversation in his office that first week. "Al's got a mean streak in him. Likes to push his weight around."

"Why put up with him, then?"

"Well, he was here when I was hired. That was ten years ago. In fact, he's been here the longest of any of us. Nearly eighteen years. He's hanging in there to get his twenty in.

Then he can get a city pension."

"Seems weird," I commented. "Unfair."

"Well, maybe..." Lou let his voice trail off and gazed out the window. "We only have you and me and Al and a couple of part timers to run the water side of this place." Lou sighed. "The thing is, Al knows his stuff. He's especially good fixing pumps and pipes. Like at the pumping stations." Residential sewage moved through the community via an underground piping system. Pumps throughout the system kept everything flowing. Any breakdown was catastrophic, and usually caused the entire system to shut down. This could eventually result in no water being supplied to the city's residents, and that would not be good. "Just watch out for him and try to avoid him if you can. Any issues," he gave me a hard look, "come to me. I've been trying to fire him for a long time now."

So, for the entire short time I had been working, I'd done just that, tried to keep my head down. But, like Lou said, the department was small so not all interactions could be avoided. I had to deal with Al to a certain extent every day, which was hard because he was one of those guys who was friendly one moment but could just as quickly turn on you and stab you in the back the next.

One time, when I was out on the cat-walk surrounding one of the separator tanks, I was on my knees reaching down fill a jar so I could conduct some tests. The tanks were deep and the effluent in them was filled with every disgusting thing you could image that people would flush down their toilets, plus a lot of stuff that you couldn't imagine as well. Al had come up from behind and slapped me hard on the back causing me to pitch forward and nearly fall in. Which wouldn't have been a good thing. In addition to everything else, the separators were filled with the raw sewage that first came into the facility. Taking a dive into it was not recommended for a multitude of reasons, primarily one's health. Al had apologized at the time and tried to laugh it off, saying he was just wanting to say hi, but I had the distinct feeling he would have been happy to see me fall in. And, if he did, whether or not he would have helped me out would have been anybody's guess.

So, now, here he was acting strange and somewhat threatening again.

"So, what are you doin'?" Al's sunglasses were propped up on the rim of his dirty Public Works baseball cap. His face was covered with beard stubble and there was a small piece of food stuck on his chin. He took a step closer. I did my best to stand firm and stay professional.

"I'm just getting a sample here for the final Biological Oxygen Demand test." BODs were run regularly to make sure the treatment process was proceeding like it should. It was one of the many tests that Al, when he was supposed to be doing them, wasn't doing. I felt I had to tip-toe around this issue. Something, frankly, I was getting sick of doing.

Then, for some reason, Al start making fun of me, mimicking my gestures, and making his voice rise higher. "Doing your precious BODs, are you?" He gave me a hard, mean look. "Sucking up to the boss man is more like it."

He took another step toward me. I was getting sick of his idiotic attitude and held my ground. "Back off, man," I said, putting my hand up to stop him. "I've got work to do."

51

"Big man, aren't you, with your precious work." Al was bigger than me and had an ample gut. He stood so close; I could smell his rank sweat soaking through his khaki work shirt. He leaned in and sneered, "You and Mr. Boss Man making nice-nice with each other?"

I had no idea where the guy came up with some of the things he said. I stared at him. "I'm just doing my job, Al. Why don't you get out of here and go do yours?" My heart rate was going up, and my breathing was getting short, a result of being both mad and scared. I didn't like either feeling.

Al stared at me a few long moment. Then he said, "Yeah, we'll see about that." He punched a finger at my chest, grinned and then turned and sauntered off through the door, taking a moment to put his sunglass on before walking out into the glare of the bright sun.

I looked after him, trying to calm down, wondering what the heck his problem was. One thing was for sure, it was obvious Al didn't care for me, not one little bit. I took a moment and collected my thoughts. Should I tell Lou about this or not? I thought about for a minute and then decided, nah, why bring it up? Al was one of those guys who was just a jerk. There wasn't much anyone could do about it. Maybe he'd eventually push things too far, then Lou would have grounds to fire him. Until then, well, I'd just have to figure out a way to live with him being around, and also get my work done. Knowing Al was not happy with me being there gave me a bit of a kick, though. The guy was an idiot and deserved whatever he ended up getting, whatever that might be.

I took a deep breath and let it out and tried to put Al out

of my mind. I wasn't going anywhere anytime soon. I had a job to do. Lou and I had to present the results of my lab tests to the MPCA later that summer in August, so I had a lot of work to do until then.

I left the building and closed the door. Once outside I looked around for Al. Surprisingly, I saw his pickup truck parked out on the county road by the entrance to the facility. It was just sitting there, engine idling. I got the distinct feeling he was watching me as I walked all the way back to my lab. It was a bit unsettling."

***

Jeremy quit reading and looked at Ebar. "I have to say, this is a pretty good story."

Ebar smiled and took a drink of water. "Thanks. I've always tried to make this and my other communiques kind of entertaining as well as informative. Especially for commander Zenon." Ebar chuckled. "He's got a short attention span."

"You use mental telepathy to communicate, right?"

"Right. I need a quiet place or at least a place I can focus. Then I basically read the message to myself to send it out. Kind of like you're doing now."

"But he never responded to this one, right?"

"That's right. I never heard a thing. I have no idea if he even received it or not." Ebar's expression turned sad, and he was quiet for a moment. Then he sighed and said, "I've heard nothing from him since before I even took the job. I don't know what's going on."

Jeremy took a drink of water. "We'll cross that bridge when we get it, okay? For now, let's keep going through this." Jeremy drank again. "Thirsty," he said.

Eber laughed. "Yeah, I had a lot to say. A lot of ground to cover."

Jeremy put down his water bottle. "I hear you. Okay, let's get back to the story."

Chapter Six

JEREMY CONTINUED READING:

"Once back in the lab, I actually forgot all about Al because I was focused on running tests on the water sample from the effluent holding tank. When I was done, I sat down and reviewed the notebook where I kept my records. The MPCA in conjunction with the MWC set the testing standards for various of Minnesota's cities and municipalities. Fortunately for me, they were based on the Federal Environmental Protection Agency's standards which were published in the thick handbook I had purchased in preparation for interviewing for my job. I kept a hard copy of my results in my notebook, and also on an old but serviceable laptop computer Lou had supplied me. There were at least thirty separate tests that had to be run every week. Many of them had forms that needed to be filled out. The test results had to be organized and kept for easy viewing by anyone who wanted to see what I was doing.

All of the tests and procedures I instituted were new to the public works department, and none of them had been done by Al. It was a full-time job, and I occasionally even worked up to four hours on Saturday or Sunday. Sometimes both. I didn't mind, though, because I felt I was doing something good for the community and that made me feel worthwhile.

Lou gave me some time to prove myself. Then one day at the beginning of June, a few weeks after the run-in with Al at the water works building, he came up to me on a Friday at the end of the day and invited me out for a beer after work.

"Time to celebrate, Kyle," he said, smiling and slapping me affectionately on the back. "You're doing a great job."

Commander Zenon, I have to say that his praise made me feel good. It was great to know I was working out and doing the kind of job Lou expected me to do. So, I agreed to go. I can't stand the alcohol flavored drinks here on earth, although they have a non-alcoholic drink called Coke that is pretty good. But I had a feeling this was about something other than drinking, and I was right. It had to with what they call bonding which means getting close to someone. Or people. Anyway, that's what we did that night. Lou drove and we went to The Hitchin' Post, a country western bar twenty miles away in the town of Southfield. There were some other employees from public works there, and we all sat around and talked. They had their drinks, and I had my coke, and it was fun. I had a good time and got home around three in the morning, feeling great. It was nice to get to know Lou better and some of the other guys, too, and to become, as Lou put it, 'Part of the team.' It felt really good.

June faded into July. The Fourth of July came and went. The crew at the public works department settled into the day-to-day tasks common to maintaining a community during the heat of the summer. In addition to watching over the pumping system, Al and the two part-timers spent a lot of time out cutting grass along the miles and miles of Orchard Lake's roadside ditches. They also filled up a five-hundred-gallon tanker truck and used it to water young trees that had been planted over the last few years along roads throughout the county.

The crew was so busy, in fact, that Al had no time to bully me, and, for my part, I pretty much forgot about him and his veiled threats. Instead, I focused on doing my job. I was past my three-month probationary period, and Lou only touched base with me once a day or so. When he came into the lab for a quick visit, I'd show him whatever test I was performing. He always seemed interested.

It was during one of those visits toward the end of July that Lou mentioned something. "I got a request from the council this morning. They want me and you to come to their next meeting and give them an update on the tests you've been running."

"Why? What's going on?" I asked. I immediately started

to get nervous. Speaking in front of people was not something I'd be comfortable doing. "Am I doing something wrong?"

"Not at all. Relax. It's just that next month some representatives from the MPCA are going to meet with the council. That's when we'll present our testing procedure and our test results. If all is A-Okay, which I'm sure it is," Lou paused and gave me a quick smile, "then everyone will be happy. The council just wants a preview of what to expect at the big meeting next month." Lou used finger quotes around big meeting. I laughed nervously.

"I've got my records in my notebook and on the computer," I said, wondering how I was ever going to get through the meeting. The Orchard Lake City Council was made up of the mayor and seven other elected officials. They held a monthly meeting in the community room just down the hall from Lou's office. Lou usually attended and knew all the members very well.

"I'll do the talking. You just organize your records so I can present them. If I can't answer any of their questions, I'll have you do it." He looked at me (I was starting to perspire) and winked. "Hey, man, don't worry. It'll be okay."

"Easy for you to say."

Lou reached over and clasped my shoulder. "Seriously, don't sweat it. We'll be fine."

After Lou left, I sat down with my notebook and reviewed my records. Everything was in order. I imagined appearing before the council and felt slightly nauseous. At least Lou would be there. Maybe everything would be fine. I sure hoped so.

During the next week, in addition to doing my tests, I organized my procedures so that Lou could easily present the results. I had a summary sheet which I used to make a spread sheet showing each test I did on each particular day of the week. The summary sheets showed how each week's results fell well within the guidelines set by the MPCA. I put all of my test results into a PowerPoint presentation for Lou to use, and then showed him how to present the information using the office laptop.

After I was done showing him everything, Lou was impressed. "I knew you could do it, Kyle. This looks great."

And it did if I did say so myself. Now, if I didn't have to say anything at the council meeting, I'd be fine.

In fact, I was feeling good about life. I liked my job, and Lou and I got along well. But then, after the flurry of summertime mowing and watering, Al started hanging around the public works building and grounds more often. "Got to look over those pumps," was what he'd say to Lou when asked about it. Which was true. Keeping the pumps up and running kept the sewage and wastewater moving through the system, and Al was not only good at maintaining them, but he was also the only guy who really knew where all of them were located. From my point of view, I tried to avoid being anywhere near him. Sometimes that couldn't be avoided, though.

The public works facility was out in the country about a mile from town and covered about twenty acres. It was enclosed by a chain link fence. At the back of the property there was an eighteen-inch vertical pipe that went straight down ten feet to where the raw sewage came into the system to begin its treatment process in the facility. Every morning I lowered a container into it to collect a sample to run tests for suspended solids and other organic compounds. The ground around the sampling pipe was low and sunken and usually damp. It also had a rank, rotten egg smell, which you got used to after a while, but it was still not pleasant.

One morning I was preoccupied, thinking, like I always did, about being careful around the pipe as I approached it, when all of a sudden Al appeared.

"Hey there, buddy'," he said, mimicking a familiar greeting of Lou's. "What are ya' up to'?"

"Geez, man. What are you doing here?" I asked, hoping I wasn't coming across as startled as was felt. Al was wearing mirrored sunglasses and chewing on a toothpick. He looked mean.

"Just checking up on ya' and those tests of yours." He paused, considering. "Hear you and the boss man have a meeting to go to."

"Yeah, so what?" I was getting sick of being intimidated by the guy. "I've got my job to do, and you've got yours. What of it?" I stood up straight, conscious of feeling like I was holding my ground.

Al took a menacing step toward me, pointing a finger. "Just don't get too big for those britches of yours, pal'," he said, poking at my chest. "You aren't all that special. I used to do those tests, too, ya' know."

"And look where it got us," I said, pushing his hand away. "Now the MPCA is watching over us. Nice mess you got us into."

Al laughed and spat out his toothpick. "Not my fault."

He gave me a challenging look. "Not my fault at all," he added, as he turned and started to walk away.

I stood watching and wondering if I should push it with him or not. Al had his facts wrong. It really was his fault that the MPCA was watching over us. Al was an idiot and had screwed up the tests. I was sick of him, sick of being intimidated by him, and sick of feeling like I always needed to watch my back whenever he was around.

Under my breath I muttered, "Yeah, well it is your fault, ya' big jerk."

But Al didn't hear it. He just sauntered away, acting like he owned the place. I turned and lowered the container into the pipe to obtain the sample. Something made me look back over my shoulder. Al was gone, but I felt the guy was still somewhere out there, watching me. I sighed to myself. Maybe next time I'll confront the creep. This crap had gone long enough."

***

Jeremy stopped reading and took a sip of water. "This is pretty good stuff," he said.

"Thanks. It was getting pretty weird there with Al."

Jeremy shuffled the papers. "But this is all you wrote."

Ebar turned red. "Yeah. That's as far as I got. When I sent the communique that night, I didn't get an immediate response but didn't think too much of it. Those kinds of things occasionally happened. After all it was a long way away to Rykos."

Jeremy nodded. "That's for sure." He leaned forward. "But go on. Then what happened? Did you quit sending?"

"No! Not on your life. I sent every day after that for about a week, but still heard nothing back. It started to get disconcerting. What was going on with Zenon? It made me nervous. Anxious."

"I definitely can understand that." Jeremy paused, thinking. Then he asked, "Even now, there's still no word I take it?"

"Nothing."

Jeremy was thoughtful. "Well, we'll get back to that. But for now, going back to the situation at the treatment plant, the more I think about it, the more I think that you really were justified getting into it with Al. I think most people would agree with you and what you did. I sure do."

"That's very kind. Thank you."

"If that was all there was to it, that'd be one thing. But then there was that issue in jail with you talking to Commander Zenon."

Ebar blushed. "I know. I think that kind of sealed my fate." He was quiet for a minute, then said, "You know, I've never told anyone this before."

Jeremy perked up and looked over. "What?"

"I finished writing my communique."

"You did?"

"Yep. Right up to the end. To the fight."

"Including the fight?"

"Yeah."

"Ebar!" Jeremy implored. "Why didn't you tell me?"

Ebar shrugged. "Well, it's been a hectic month or so. I've been arrested and stuck in jail. Then they'd put me in the loony-bin in the hospital. Now here." He pointed around the room. "I've had time on my hands, so I wrote it up. I just finished last week." He got to his feet, went to his desk, and took out some more papers. He held them out to Jeremy. "Here they are. Want to read them?"

Jeremy shot out his hand and took them before Ebar could change his mind. "You bet! Of course, I do."

Ebar smiled gratefully. "Thank you." He went back, sat on the bed, and lay back against the wall. "Might as well make myself comfortable." He unscrewed the cap and took a drink from his water bottle. "This is where it gets interesting."

Chapter Seven

JEREMY TOOK A swig of water and began reading:

"The following week was when the council met to review my testing procedures. It was scheduled for Tuesday, August 10th. The sky was gray and cloudy, and by the time the meeting started at 4:00 pm rain had started. There was one final water sample for the day that I had to collect, but Lou told me to wait until after the meeting, so I did.

All in all, the presentation went fine. The mayor, Betsy

Williams, was on her fourth term and was very well liked both by the council and the citizens of Orchard Lake. Lots of people felt it was due to her leadership that the community was as thriving and prosperous as it was. So, when Lou finished his presentation to an enthusiastic round of applause lead by the mayor, I was able to breathe a sigh of relief. She opened the floor up to questions, some of which Lou could answer and a few that he deferred to me, which I handled pretty well. I surprised myself by being hardly nervous at all.

After fifteen minutes, there were no further questions, and the meeting was adjourned. Lou introduced me to the council members I hadn't met yet, and then the two of us went out to the hallway.

Lou put his arm around my shoulder in a rare show of affection. "You did good, Kyle. Really good. I'm proud of you." He was smiling broadly. "How about if we head down to The Hitchin' Post for a celebration?" He was as happy as I'd had ever seen him. The pressure exerted by the Minnesota Pollution Control Agency had been weighing heavily on him, and the first step had successfully been taken. Now, in two weeks, all we had to do was to present my test results to the MPCA and we'd be fine. The ordeal was almost over.

I had no desire to go out to celebrate, but I understood Lou's enthusiasm and didn't want to do anything to dampen it. "I'd love to go, but first let me run this last test."

Lou was getting ready to argue when some of the council members stopped by and agreed to join him for drinks and celebration. I got the feeling it would eventually turn into a long night and was happy to have the excuse of doing some work so I wouldn't have to go.

"I admire your commitment to your job," Lou grinned and clapped me on the shoulder. "I'll give you a rain check until next time."

"Thanks." I told him, and, pointed outside where it was thundering lightning like crazy. "Speaking of rain, you guys be careful out there."

After bidding me good-bye, Lou and the others headed for Lou's truck while I went into my lab to grab my collection bottle and put on my raincoat and hat. The storm had intensified, and as I pushed out the door the wind blew my hat off. I ran to get it and stuffed it in my pocket. It'd do me no good in this weather. Cold rain pelted my face, and the wind whipped my coat like it was made of tissue paper.

"Man. I should have just forgotten about the test and gone to the bar with the others," I muttered myself. "At least then I'd be comfortable and dry."

I looked around the parking lot. Everyone had left, and I was all by myself. Way out to the west was a flash of lightening followed by rolling thunder. I sighed, pulled my raincoat close, put up my hood and started toward the entrance gate. It took about ten minutes to get there, slopping through muddy puddles along the way, water soaking my boots, rain running into my eyes.

Finally, I made it. To the right of the entrance gate about twenty feet off the road, right up by the fence was a storm sewer. A heavy metal grate nearly four feet across covered it. With some difficulty and using both hands, I pulled the lid up and propped it in place with a metal rod that was attached to it for just that purpose. I looked into the drain.

Water was rushing through a large transfer pipe twelve feet down. I had to climb down to it using metal latter rungs on the side of the wall, something I wasn't looking forward to doing. The metal rungs would be wet, and my hands could slip on them. Or my boots. It was dangerous and my least favorite job I had to do. But the MPCA required a sample of the storm sewage runoff during a heavy rain, so there was no choice. I had to do it.

Lightning flashed some more, and thunder boomed. If possible, it started raining even harder. I spent a moment psyching himself up for the task ahead, then stepped into the pipe. Moving cautiously, I started down the ladder, taking my time and carefully placing my boots and hands on the rungs as I lowered myself into the hole. In a few minutes I was down to the bottom rung where the water was rushing past about a foot below my boots. Holding onto the ladder with one hand, I took the sampling bottle out of my pocket, squatted down, scooped up a sample and snapped the top back on.

I was just straightening up when a loud noise from above startled me so badly I almost dropped my sampling container. I quickly put it in my jacket pocket and secured the flap. Then I looked up, and what I saw made my stomach turn over. The grate had come crashing down. I was trapped.

Quickly, but cautiously, I climbed up to the top of the ladder and used my shoulder to push against the grate, trying to lift it. Nothing happened. It wouldn't budge. I looked back down into the pipe, and to my horror the level of the storm sewer water was starting to rise. I momentarily wondered why that would be happening. The only thing causing it would be a pump being out somewhere down the line. I quickly made the connection. Al. It must be him. He must have disabled one of the downstream pumps. That's what could create a blockage causing the water to back up. It eventually would fill up the pipe I was in and spill out through the grate. Even though rain runoff was coming in through the bars up above and dripping onto my face, I broke out into a cold sweat. Unless I could escape, I'd drown.

I took out my phone to call for help but the bars were flat. I had no signal and swore loud and long, "Damn! Damn! Damn!"

The pipe I was in was about four feet across, the same diameter as the grate that was trapping me, but it suddenly felt like I was in a tomb, narrow and claustrophobic. I looked down over my shoulder. The water was a churning, foaming, brownish mess as it rose up toward me. It was filled with debris that banged against the side of pipe. I had to get out!

I used my feet to brace myself on one of the ladder rungs. Then I grabbed the bars of the grate with one hand and, using my upper back and shoulder, pushed up with all my might. It gave ever so slightly. Yea! I might be able to get it open, but I had to hurry.

I looked back down into the pipe. The water was level with my boots and rising fast. I noticed branches and other debris floating in the miasma, so I got a hold of a stick, and then used my shoulder to push up against the grate again. It moved just a bit more, enough so I was able to jam the stick under the lip. It wasn't much, but it was something.

The exertion left me panting. Sweat was pouring off me

and running into my eyes. My hands were bloody from pushing against the metal bars on the grate. I took a moment to gather my strength. I could feel the water rising and roaring, echoing in the pipe. It was above my boots now. I was jammed up on the top rungs with my knees bent beneath me. Through the grate I could see the gray sky and freedom. I wiggled the end of the branch like a lever. The grate moved a little more. At least it wasn't stuck, and it gave me hope.

I figured I had just enough strength for one final push. The water was rising fast and had come up above my knees to my thighs. I forced one hand under the edge of the grate by where the stick was, and, with my other hand and shoulder, forced my way up, pushing with all my might with my legs. My muscles screamed as the grate lifted a little more. That's all it took. Adrenaline flooded my body, and I pushed one last time, yelling out loud, "Ahhhh!" The grate lifted and fell away, and I fell with it, my momentum carrying my body half out of the opening. Just then the storm sewer water burst from the pipe flooding the ground around me. I had made it just in time. I was free.

I took a moment to gather my strength, and then climbed the rest of the way out of the hole. On my hands and knees, I crawled through the sloppy water to where the ground was a little higher, about ten feet away. Water was flowing out of the storm sewer forming an ever-widening pool. I got into a sitting position and stared at it. The rain was still pouring down. I was soaked and shaken, but safe and alive.

I was just starting to think about getting up and heading back to the lab when something caused me to look over my

70

shoulder. Through the sheets of pouring rain, I saw a pickup truck parked about fifty feet away. I knew right away that it wasn't just any pickup truck; it was Al's.

I leaped to my feet. My vision flashed to being almost drowned in the sewer pipe and a fury roared through my body like a runaway freight train. Then everything went blank for an instant, one tiny moment, before my brain exploded. I literally saw red, a fiery rage so powerful that all of the fatigue I felt was suddenly replaced by a hatred so strong that it flooded my body, surging through my muscles in a torrent a thousand times more powerful than mightiest river.

While I was looking at his truck, Al calmly rolled down the window and gave me the finger. Then he started laughing. He might have said something, too, but, if he did, I had no idea what it was. He rolled the window back up, and I heard the engine rev as the truck started to move away from me. I couldn't let him get away.

Frantically, I looked around. Nearby was a fist sized rock. I picked it up, ran after the truck and heaved it with all my might. It smashed into the driver's side window, spider-webbing the glass. *Direct hit*, I thought to myself. *Got him good*.

The truck jolted to a stop, and Al opened the door. Whatever he was planning on doing he never got the chance. Mad beyond all comprehension, I sprinted, covering the distance between us in a split second. I leaped at Al as he was trying to step from the cab and grabbed him by his jacket. I pulled him all the way out and smashed his head against the side of the truck. There was a sicken 'thud' as the bigger man slumped to the ground momentarily stunned. He tried to get up, but he was no match for me. I'll tell you, Commander Zenon, I've never be so mad in my life. My anger exploded as I fell on him, beating on the creep until he was bleeding from his mouth and nose. I stopped when it was apparent he'd lost consciousness, lying motionless on his back as rainwater rivulets mixed with the blood running off his face. He wasn't going anywhere. I got up and dragged the body to the pool forming around the storm sewer pipe. I'd never felt stronger in my entire life.

Al started to come to as I pulled him into the pool. I quickly rolled him onto his stomach and then I climbed onto his back, pushing his head under the water, drowning him. His arms started windmilling and I ducked out of the way. After about a minute, they went slack. I watched as air bubbles escaped through his nostrils. He was still breathing, but not for long. I'd had it with his verbal abuse, and him treating me like I was nothing but a punching bag for his bullying behavior. He was a jerk and worth nothing in my book. All I wanted to do at that moment was to kill the guy.

But I didn't. In the end, as I held the limp body submerged under the filthy water, I had a change of heart. To this day, I'm not sure what it was, but all of a sudden, I had a vision, not of dirty storm sewer water with god only knew what kind of crap and debris floating in it, but of something else. I saw the crystal-clear waters of my youth and being at the reservoir with my mom, walking along the shore and talking, being together and enjoying the day and the simple fact of being alive. And not just one day, either, but many days, with the sun shining brightly and the birds calling and soaring above us. And it was all good.

Those images flashed into my brain in an instant. And,

in that moment, I realized that I didn't need to do what I felt I had to do, which was to drown Al. No. I'd made my point. I'd beaten the guy up and made him pay for trapping me in that storm sewer. Now I was done with him.

I sat back on my heels, caught my breath, and then stood up, pulling the limp body from the water. I dragged Al away from the pool to some higher ground. Then rolled him on his back and used chest compressions to force water from his lungs. In a few seconds he coughed and threw up about a gallon of water. Then he rolled to his side gasping.

It was at this point I was aware of another truck driving toward me. I look up. It was Lou. He skidded to a stop in the mud, got out of his truck and ran to us. The rain was still beating down, and water was bubbling out of the sewer in a fountain at least three feet high. He took one look at the two of us on the ground, and then made his decision. Al was okay, just coughing and trying to stand up. Lou went to him to help, as I got my feet and waited, wondering what my boss was going to do with the two of us.

I didn't have to wait long. What Lou did was to take charge. "What the hell, you jerk," he shouted, shaking Al within an inch of his life. The wind had picked up and almost carried his voice away, but I could still hear him. "What the hell have you been up to?"

Al glanced back at me. I met him eye to eye, challenging him, daring him to say something, anything. But Al averted my gaze. "Nothin'," he spat out, pulling away from Lou and trying to walk away. "Not a damn thing."

Lou grabbed him by the back of his shirt and turned him around, so they were face to face. "I'd think about that if I were you," Lou said, and gave him another shake. "I got an emergency call. Something's caused that sewer to back up, and I think that something is a someone, and I think that someone is you." He pulled Al to his truck and roughly forced him in. Al had gone quiet, seemingly resigned to his fate. "Stay here," Lou commanded.

Then he came back to me. "Climb in back and let's get to the lab," he ordered. Then he looked more closely at me and seemed to notice something. He relaxed his tone and patted me on the back. "You can fill me in on what went on here later. Okay? Right now, I've got a pump to fix."

I climbed into the back of the truck, and we headed for the lab. I was shivering, not from the cold rain, but from the release of adrenaline. The rain had washed my hands free of blood, but they were shaking badly. I flexed them. They were sore, but no bones appeared to have been broken. I looked into the cab through the back window and saw Al slumped in his seat up against the passenger side door. He looked defeated. *Good*, I thought to myself. *It's about time.*

Back at the lab Lou took Al into his office, and whatever he did or said in there worked. In five minutes, they both came out and headed for the door. "We're going to go and fix that pump," he said to me on the way out. "Go home and dry out. Be back here by 7:00 am tomorrow. We'll talk then." Then he pushed Al through the door, and they were gone.

I went into my lab and looked around. On the desk was my notebook with my test results. There was also a copy of the presentation I'd put together for Lou. I sat down, suddenly exhausted. I cradled my head in my arms on my desk and rested, thinking about the fight with Al and how I'd nearly let my emotions take over. I'd come just that close to drowning the guy. All the good things I'd ever felt about being around water almost vanished when I remembered what it felt like to hold Al under that pool bubbling up from the storm sewer and watching the life slowly drain out him.

I sat up quickly, shook my head, clearing his mind, and then got to my feet. I looked around my lab one more time, and then turned out the light. I walked outside into the early evening. The rain was starting to let up. Out to the west through a crack in the clouds, sunlight was pouring through. Tomorrow was another day. I had a feeling Lou would side with me if it came down to it. Al was not someone my boss wanted to keep around anyway. Maybe this would be the opportunity he had been waiting for to get rid of the guy.

Whatever...I suddenly didn't really care about all of that. I was wet, I was cold, I was shivering and beyond exhausted. I needed to get home and clean up, dry out and warm up. Tomorrow was another day. I wanted to be ready for it."

***

Jeremy quit reading, set the paper on Ebar's desk, and said, "Well, that's it."

"Yeah, it is. What do you think?"

"I have to say that it's a heck of a story."

"Well, the next day the cops came to work and took me away. Al had pressed charges."

"Yeah, I read that in the report." He looked at Ebar. "I also read that the meeting with the MPCA went well.

Orchard Lake is in the clear now. That's because of you."

Embarrassed at the compliment, Ebar blushed. "Thank you, but it's all kind of pointless now." He waved his hand around his tiny room. 'I'm sorry all of this happened."

Jeremy tried to console him. "I really don't think it should have gotten to this. I think you were justified in beating up Al. You would have probably been found not guilty."

"You think so?"

"I know so."

They were both quiet for a minute. Then Ebar said, "Except…"

"Except you opened you mouth and mentioned your commander. Commander Zenon."

"Yeah, I know. I shouldn't have done that."

"But you did, and that means there's a witness."

"The jailer."

"Yeah."

"What should we do?"

"We've got to come up with a plan."

Ebar sat forward, ready to pay attention. "A plan. You mean you think you can help me?"

"I do. But let me ask you this. What do you want out of all of this." Jeremy pointed to Ebar and then to himself. "Me and you. Our counseling sessions. Talking. What's the end result you're looking for?"

Ebar thought for a minute and then said. "Well, what I'd

really like is for people to believe that I'm an alien and not just some crazy person. I'm sick of living a lie. I'd like people to know the truth. That's what I'd really like."

Jeremy was stunned. Even though they'd skirted the issue in the past, they'd never really talked about it until now. In a way, Jeremy almost wished he hadn't brought it up. But he had, and now the cards were on the table. "You know what you're asking, right? You're asking people who have rational scientific minds to put aside their beliefs and accept, beyond all logic, that you came to earth from another planet in another galaxy and have been living here for fifty years." Jeremy looked hard at Ebar. "That's asking a lot. You know that don't you?"

Ebar returned Jeremy's gaze and said, "I know it is, but it's the truth. And the truth is a good thing, right? So, why not tell people that?"

Jeremy was touched by Ebar's honesty, misplaced and naïve though it may be. But he had to bite back the words *because it's insane* and, instead, said, "Well, if that's what you want, I'll do everything I can to help you." Inside his chest, his heart was pounding like a drum. What had he just agreed to do? He had no idea what he was going to do to help his patient.

Ebar jumped his feet. "You will! That's fantastic. What are we going to do?"

Jeremy quickly looked away, gathering himself before he answered. "Oh, I've got a couple of ideas."

"Great, let's hear them."

Jeremy checked his watch. He had to get out of there and do some serious thinking. "I'd love to go over them right now, but our time together today has run really long, and I need to get going."

Disappointed, Ebar said, "Oh."

"Look, tomorrow's Friday, and I can come back then, okay? I know you're free after your group session. I'll see you after lunch."

"Okay," he said, quietly. Subdued. Then he had a sudden thought and grinned. "In fact, that's great. I'm looking forward to hearing what you come up with."

"Super. We'll talk then."

Jeremy forced a smile, shook Ebar's hand and left the room. He walked down the hall, down the stairs and out the front door of the group home into the bright sunshine, all the time thinking, *Man, Ebar's depending on me to help him, but what am I going to do? Because, honestly, right now, I don't have a clue.*

Chapter Eight

LATER THAT NIGHT, Julie Brooks and her partner Wren Lindstrom were in the kitchen preparing their evening meal. There was a scent of fresh basil in air from the pesto Wren had made earlier. She was of average height and build, and partial to wearing jeans and oversized tee-shirts. Her hair was a mass of dark curls she cut herself, which framed an oval face made distinctive by one-inch round red birthmark on her left cheek. She worked at home as a graphic arts designer and had her studio in the basement. Julie had an appreciation of art and the two of them were looking forward dinner and conversation and a relaxing Thursday at home, catching up on the events of their day.

Julie's phone buzzed with a text message.

Wren was putting together a tossed salad and asked, "Who's that?"

Julie paused stirring the noodles for spaghetti and looked. "It's my friend from work I've told you about. Jeremy."

"Ah, yes. The bearded man. Well, dinner's almost ready. What do you think he wants?"

"I'm not sure, but I'm pretty sure I've got a guess. I'll bet has to do with what he and I talked about at the coffee shop yesterday. You know, after the Wednesday meeting."

"Yeah, I remember. You said he was into some interesting stuff with his patient, but that you couldn't go into specifics." She chided her partner and nudged her with an elbow. "You and your patient privilege." Wren set about slicing some tomatoes for the salad. "Do you think it's important?"

"Must be if he's calling like this."

Wren sighed and set down her paring knife. "Better answer it then. Dinner can wait."

"You're a dream."

"Always, lover." Wren smiled and poured a glass of white wine, gave it to Julie, and then poured one for herself. She pointed to Julie's phone. "What are you waiting for? Hurry up and call him. Now I'm curious."

Julie turned the burner down to let the noodles simmer and did just that.

Jeremy answered right away. He sounded frazzled. "Julie. Thank you so much for getting back to me."

"I just got your text. What's going on?"

"It's about Ebar. I'm trying to figure out what to do."

"Like I told you yesterday afternoon. Remember patient confidentiality. It's a serious thing you know."

"I know, but he told me it's okay if I run a few things by you."

"He did?"

"Yeah. Even though he hasn't met you, he knows I respect your opinion. That's good enough for him."

"Hmm. You sure?"

"Yes. I promise. I'll have him sign something if you want."

Julie chuckled. "That won't be necessary. We'll just call this a consultation. How's that sound."

Jeremy breathed an audible sigh of relief and said, "That'd be great. I could use you as a sounding board."

Julie took a sip of wine and said, "I'm happy to do what I can. Just give me just a second."

Julie was forty-one-years old and had been a mental health professional for sixteen years. She loved her work and enjoyed the day-to-day interaction with her patients. Like Jeremy, she refused to call them clients. Over the last few years, she'd gravitated toward hospice care, and now specialized in one-on-one counseling for those in need at the end of their life; patients and their families alike. She enjoyed the work, and had an aptitude for it, but in thinking of Jeremy and his patient, she could see herself helping out. It might be fun. Different, anyway.

She covered the mouthpiece. "Wren, this might be a while."

Wren sighed, good-naturedly. "Okay." She turned off the burner on the spaghetti, then kissed Julie on the cheek. "Do your thing, babe."

Julie smiled. The two of them lived in a small cottage style home in south Minneapolis, about 40 miles from the hospital in Ryerson. She and Wren had been together for twenty years and had been married for the last six. They'd bought the house as a wedding gift to themselves. It was on a small lot with a shady backyard and patio, and that's where Julie went to talk with Jeremy. She also had the half a glass of white wine Wren had given her as she'd gone out the backdoor.

Getting settled in a comfortable Adirondack chair, Julie said, "Alright, I'm outside in the back where it's private. Why don't you tell me what's going on?"

Then she listened to Jeremy as he talked for nearly ten minutes, mostly about what he'd learned that day about the fight at the sewage treatment plant, something Julie had not heard the specifics of before. In fact, Jeremy talked so much and so fast, he never gave her a chance to get a word in. The overriding thought forming in Julie's mind as she listened was that Jeremy was a kind and caring person, and he was obviously committed to helping his patient. The mental health field could use more like him.

Jeremy finally stopped talking, and she could hear him take a drink. *Probably water,* she thought to herself. She'd noticed in the month or so that she'd known him that Jeremy drank a lot of water. *What's up with that?* It made her thirsty just thinking about it. She took a grateful sip of wine and said, "Okay, so let me recap what I heard you say."

"Go ahead."

"I know the background of Kyle, based on what you told us yesterday at the group meeting."

"Right."

"Kyle…"

"Um, Julie? Sorry to interrupt, but could you call him Ebar? Just for now?"

"But he's Kyle."

"I know." Jeremy was obviously frustrated. "He's Kyle. He's Ebar. He's both. He's…"

"Hold on, Jeremy. Just calm down. Maybe you should tell me why you called me in the first place."

She heard him sigh in the background, followed by another drink of water. Then, he said, "Here's the thing. Remember that I've got to present my case at the meeting next Wednesday."

"Right."

"Ebar wants me to prove to them he's an alien."

There was a long moment of silence before Julie exclaimed, "Good lord!"

Her voice was so loud, for a second Jeremy had to hold the phone away from his ear. Then he said, "Crazy, isn't it?"

Julie took a healthy swig of wine to give herself a

moment to collect herself. *Crazy was putting it mildly*, she thought to herself. Then she remembered something. "What a minute. Yesterday when we talked at the coffee shop, you told me you were unsure about him, and whether or not he was an alien. Now here you are telling me he wants you to prove that he is one? What's going on? Has something changed?"

Dead silence. Then, "Well…Yes."

Julie got right to the point. "You made a decision about him, didn't you? Better tell me what it is. I've got to know the truth to help you."

"I know. It's just all of this is so new to me. I grew up on a farm. I spent more time with dairy cows than humans. I wasn't ready for this. I got into counseling to help people. People, not aliens! I never thought I'd be in the situation I'm in now."

Julie laughed softly, hoping to ease the tension for Jeremy. She liked the kindhearted young counselor. "Welcome to the real world."

"Tell me about it."

"So, what's up? What'd you decide?"

Jeremy took a deep breath and let it out. Then he said, "I've come to the conclusion that he is what he says he is. An alien, I mean."

Julie choked on the wine she'd just sipped. Even though she thought that's what he might say, hearing it spoken out loud was something else again. She coughed to clear her throat. When she got control, she said, "You're kidding, right?"

"No," he said, quietly. "I really mean it."

"I don't understand."

"It kind of got down to the communiques he wrote. I've looked through a bunch of them. They're very authentic. They mention Commander Zenon and the planet Rykos. There's no way he could make that stuff up. Well, he could, obviously, but he's just so sincere. So real. And now, since there's been no communication between him and the commander, he's not only lonely for his home planet, but scared that he's been left alone with no chance to return." Jeremy went on and told her about Ebar being at the reservoir with his mom. And about the yookies. Everything he could remember Ebar had told him earlier that day. When he finished, he said, "There's just something about him, Julie." She could hear the pleading tone in Jeremy's voice for her to believe him. "He's just so honest. I don't think it's possible for him to lie."

"Everyone's capable of lying, Jeremy. Take it from me, after sixteen years in this business, I've seen it all. You want to believe the patients, you really do, but then something always happens."

"Still, I have to go with my gut."

Julie laughed, derisively. "Your gut! You're supposed to be a professional, and trained in observation and counseling, not listening to your gut. Anyone can do that."

Julie listened to the silence on the end of the line. *I probably hurt his feelings. Well, too, bad.* What she said was the truth. At least from her experience.

Finally, Jeremy said, his voice soft, but sincere, "I don't care. I believe him and I'm going to do whatever I can for

85

him. If you don't want to help, that's fine. Just tell me. I'll figure out what do with him on my own."

Julie sighed. She could tell his mind was made up. She'd been in similar situations. Not with a supposed alien, of course, but with a belief in somebody that was so strong, nothing and no one could dissuade her.

Even though he couldn't see her, Julie nodded her acceptance of her friend's situation. She'd made her decision. "Okay. I'll help."

The relief in Jeremy's voice was obvious. "Oh, Julie, that's wonderful. Thank you so much."

"This won't be easy, but you're welcome. Besides, it will be an interesting challenge, and I'm up for it. I've never helped someone help an alien before. Now, what do you want from me?"

"Not a whole lot, I don't think. I just want you to be on my side."

Julie smiled. The mental health profession could be brutal. Burn-out was high. Friendships came and went. People lost their good intentions of helping others really fast. It'd been a long time since she'd seen anyone with Jeremy's enthusiasm, naïve as it might be. Her heart went out to him. "Okay. I can do that."

"Oh, man, that's fantastic," he said, sighing with relief. "Again, thank you."

"Well, time will tell if it's *fantastic* or not," she said, "but, I'll do what I can." She paused, then asked, "So what are you going to do?"

"I've been thinking about it. I keep going back to his

water treatment communiques. I think I'm going to use them to try and show that he really is a good guy. He's just had some life issues that I can help him deal with. I'll try to show the group that, in the end, he's not crazy but a decent human being. I think I can convince Andrews and the others to leave him at the group home for continued treatment and therapy."

"Instead of sending him back to jail?"

"Yeah."

"Well, good luck." She tried not to sound too sarcastic.

Jeremy didn't even notice. "Thank you."

Julie smiled into her phone. The more she was around him, the more she liked Jeremy's positive 'can do' attitude. She said, "It's going to be hard you know. The easiest thing, and the cheapest thing, unfortunately, is to send him back to county lockup to await trial. That's what Andrews will be pushing you to do."

"Yeah, I kind of figured that."

They were quiet for a minute, then Julie asked, "So, how's Kyle, I mean Ebar, feel about all of this? Your plan is to convince everyone he's human with issues caused by life events. You're basically going to be going against his wishes. Remember, he told you he wants you to prove that he's an alien."

"I know. I don't think he's going to like it, but…"

"Don't think? Wait a minute. You mean you haven't told him?" Julie asked incredulously.

"Not really. Well, no. I just came up with the idea tonight after I thought about his situation and looked at that water treatment communique some more."

Julie shook her head. "Good lord. Well, good luck convincing him."

"Thanks. I think I'll need it."

"I'm sure you will. When are you going to see him again?"

"Tomorrow, early afternoon. In fact, I should probably get going. I've got a lot of notes to go through."

"Okay, sounds good." She paused and added, "Look, Jeremy, I know all of this is complicated. I'm glad you called. Hopefully, we can make this work out for Ebar. Keep me posted, okay?"

Jeremy was glad to hear Julie had said 'we'. He smiled into the phone and said, "I will."

***

After they hung up, Wren came out to the patio with a bottle and poured some more wine for Julie. "How'd it go?"

"Oh, not too bad," Julie said, taking a sip and shaking her head. "It's just that my friend Jeremy has bitten off more than he can chew, I'm afraid."

Wren gently rubbed Julie's arm. "Feel like talking about it?"

"How about over dinner?"

"Sounds good to me."

And after they had eaten, and after Julie had told Wren

about Jeremy's plan to convince Andrews and the others that Ebar was really Kyle who was a misguide human and not the alien he really was, even Wren, an artist who embraced all things odd, different, and radical, had to admit that it was a crazy idea.

"Well, he'll be glad he's got you on his side, babe."

Wren was washing the dinner dishes and Julie was drying them and putting them away. "Why is that?" she asked.

Wren grinned. "Because you've got me backing you up. Your friend Jeremy gets both of us. Two for the price of one."

Julie laughed. "I never thought of it that way." She hugged Wren and finished putting the last of the dishes away. "And, you know what?"

"What?"

"He may end up needed both of us."

Wren laughed, "If what you've told me is correct, and this Ebar really is an alien, all I've got to say is this…"

"What's that?"

"That you're right."

Chapter Nine

THE NEXT DAY, Friday, Jeremy spent most of the afternoon talking to Ebar laying out his strategy. He knew that his patient wasn't one-hundred percent on board with his plan to convince Andrews and the others that Ebar was really Kyle, a misguided man who'd cracked up due to life issues and beaten up one of his co-workers.

"I'll make sure to convince them that with proper guidance and counseling, I'm positive you can get better," Jeremy had reiterated time and time again.

They'd agreed that he would try to convince the others that Ebar thinking he was an alien was an illusion triggered by the horrifying experience of nearly drowning in the sewer pipe during the rainstorm. Jeremy planned to go over Ebar's sewage treatment communique he'd sent to Zenon, as well as the one he had recently written but hadn't sent.

After lots of discussion, Ebar had finally agreed with Jeremy's plan saying, "I guess, when all is said and done, I really don't have much choice, do I?"

"Well, not really. It's the best I can come up with."

"If that's what we need to do to get me out of here, then, let's do it."

"I like your attitude."

They talked more on Saturday and Sunday. Monday, they took a break. Then on Tuesday, September 21st, the day before the big meeting, the two of them met in Ebar's room at the group home one more time.

Ebar sat on his bed and sipped from his water bottle. A few feet away, Jeremy made himself as comfortable as he could on the cushion-less desk chair. He glanced toward the door, or where the door would be if there had been one. There was activity out in the hall, and a steady stream of people walking by, but hardly anyone glanced at them. The patients had all learned over time to respect each other's privacy, so they studiously avoided looking in. And that included the orderlies, who by now, after five weeks, knew that Ebar and his calm demeanor was not ever going to be a problem.

Jeremy was going through his briefcase, and Ebar asked, "So, the meeting's tomorrow at ten?"

Jeremy looked up. He briefcase was on his knees, and he was meticulously going through his papers. "Yeah. Ten in the morning. Me and Andrews and Wren and Kucinen. And Julie, of course. She'll be there for sure."

"That's good."

"Yeah, it is," Jeremy said, slightly distracted.

"What are you looking for?"

"I thought you and I could review another of your communiques. Just in case."

"You really think you can pull it off?"

"Hopefully. At least I can promise you that I'm going to give it my best shot."

"It's not a bad plan that you came up with. Thank you."

Jeremy cracked a quick smile and went back to shuffling papers. "You're welcome," he said.

Ebar thought for a moment and then asked, "Did you get a chance to talk to Lou?"

"Yeah, I talked to him yesterday. Monday. He was glad I called. He sounds like a good guy."

"He is." Ebar was quiet for a moment and then asked, "Did he say why he hasn't called me?"

"Yes, it's like we thought. He was told by his lawyer that since there was going to be a court case against you for that assault charge filed by Al, he shouldn't have anything to do with you."

"Ouch. That's harsh."

"No. I mean…"

Ebar chuckled. "Hey, I was just kidding. I get it."

"Lou did tell me to tell you that he wanted to get together when this is all over. 'To celebrate like hell' was the way he put it."

Ebar smiled. "Probably at the Hitchin' Post. He likes that place a lot. He's a good guy."

"Yeah, he is. He's definitely on your side." Jeremy went back to his papers. "Oh, he says 'hi' by the way."

"Well, 'hi' right back at him," Ebar grinned. Hopefully, I see him soon."

"I guess the first hearing is in a couple of weeks. They've assigned you Leslie Anderson, a public defender. She's young, but good." Jeremy joked. "Like me."

Ebar smiled, took off his glasses and polished them with a handkerchief before putting them back on. "I know," he said. "She called me over the weekend and introduced herself. I told her about you and Wednesday's meeting. She said to keep her posted, and I told her I would. She's coming over a week from today to talk."

"That's good. We'll, have a better picture of things after tomorrow."

"I still can't convince you to prove to them I'm an alien."

Jeremy looked around frantically. "God, Ebar, don't say that! Someone might overhear. Let's just keep it simple, okay? Which will be hard enough. Trying to convince Andrews that you're suffering from a traumatic episode is easier than convincing him that you're an alien. Remember, what we want is to keep you out of jail. We want to get you feeling better and on the road to mental health recovery."

"So, I can go back to work at the treatment plant?"

Jeremy sighed a relieved sigh. "Yes. So, you can go back to work."

Ebar watch his counselor sort through his papers. He appreciated all Jeremy was doing for him, he really did. If he could stay out of jail, that'd be great. It'd be easier to try and reach Zenon from the relative peace and quiet of the group home compared to the unrelenting chaos of the jail. So, to that end, he was willing to play along. But the bigger picture loomed; what was going on with Zenon? Why the loss of contact?

Jeremy continued to sort through his papers. Finally, Ebar asked, "Say, what's up, anyway? You seem preoccupied."

Jeremy sighed, closed his briefcase, and set it on the floor. "Sorry. I guess I'm just worried about tomorrow's meeting."

"Hey, don't be. Just do like we talked about. Tell them about me working at the treatment plant. Let them know I was a good worker. Lou will attest to that."

"Yeah, he would. I'm thinking about using him for a character witness if I need to."

"Good. I'm sure he'd do it."

"It's just kind of a slippery slope, you know?"

"What do you mean?"

Jeremy looked to the empty hallway and whispered, "Well, you really are an alien."

Ebar grinned. "I am. I'm glad you've finally seen the light."

Jeremy ran his fingers nervously through his beard. "Me, too. And that's kind of the problem."

"Why's that? Seems perfectly clear to me. You make the case that I'm a normal guy who was just under a lot of stress at work due to Al, and I snapped." To emphasize his point, Ebar snapped his fingers. "Like that." He grinned. "Shouldn't be a problem."

"Yeah, I know, but here's the deal. I'm going to be lying and telling them that you really are something you aren't."

"So?"

"I'm just not a very good lair."

Which was a statement that didn't surprise Ebar at all. "Well, what can I do to help?"

"Can you tell me some more about your life here on earth? I've looked through your communiques, but I haven't really found anything as good as the sewage treatment one."

"But those were meant for commander Zenon. I don't see how they'd help us now. I mean, you're supposed to be proving to them that I'm just a deranged citizen who flipped out due to being under pressure at work."

"Right. I was thinking that I could use one of your communiques to give them a broader picture of what you're like living in Orchard Lake."

"Like maybe when I was working at the hardware store?"

"Yeah, something like that."

Ebar thought for a moment. Then he said, "Here. Give the folder with my communiques in it. I might have something in there that can help."

Jeremy handed over the folder and watched as Ebar paged through it. In a minute, he found what he was looking for.

"Let's see. I've got one in here where I helped a guy plant a garden. A few years ago, during the spring, he came in early one Saturday morning and wandered around the store kind of aimlessly. We got to talking. His whole life was devoted to working as an attorney in downtown Minneapolis. It turned out that he was spending so much time at work that he'd lost focus and thought planting a garden would help get him, as he put it, 'get back on track'. I absolutely agreed with him and helped him pick out some tools. He was pretty green to the gardening business, pun intended," Ebar grinned, "so, I told him about annuals and perennials and vegetables and compost and stuff like that and got him started. I ended up spending a lot of time over at his place on the weekends helping out."

"How'd that go?" Jeremy asked, watching as Ebar paged through the communiques, thinking that from water treatment to gardening the guy really knew a lot. It was pretty impressive.

"It went well. Eventually his wife and three young kids got involved. They had fun planting flowers and vegetables and harvesting them in the fall. The family really came together." He looked at Jeremy. "In fact, a few years later they sold their big house and moved to a smaller one. Downsized. They planted another garden and just love it. He still works as an attorney but is working less hours. The whole family is doing really well, because they realized that what's important is being together, not having a ton of possessions." Ebar looked at Jeremy and smiled. "Makes sense, doesn't it?"

Jeremy nodded. It did.

Suddenly, he mentally slapped himself across the side of the head at how stupid he was. What was he thinking about? All he had to do was focus on the incident at the treatment plant and show Andrews, Wallace, Kucinen and Julie that Ebar was pretty much as normal as anyone else. He'd just had a meltdown due to the pressure of working around Al and now needed help getting his head on straight. He could make the group see that, right?

Jeremy reached for the file. "Here, Ebar. Give that to me."

"Why? I thought you wanted some more examples."

Jeremy felt his confidence building. "Nope. We're good to go. We've got a good plan. I can pull this off."

Ebar could see a light in his counselor's eyes he hadn't seen before. A fire was burning, and it was good. He handed Jeremy the file. "You sure?"

"I am."

"Well, that's good."

"Why's that?"

"The new garden communique is good, but not as good as the sewage treatment one."

Jeremy grinned, "So, that's the one we'll use. We'll call it 'The Incident at the Sewage Treatment Plant' and make them believe you just need professional help."

"Agreed. Oh, and that I'm not an alien."

"Correct. You're not an alien."

"Even though I am."

Jeremy shook his head at the dichotomy of it all and grinned. "Right. Even though you are."

He started putting the papers back in his briefcase while Ebar smiled to himself, drank his water, and looked out the window, seemingly without a care in the world. Jeremy watched him, this quiet bespeckled man, who was now depending on him to help get his freedom back. he sighed, closed his briefcase, and took a drink of his own water, his hand shaking ever so slightly. His alien patient had complete trust in him that all would turn out well for him in the end. And not for the first time, and probably not the last, either Jeremy thought to himself, *what have I gotten myself into?*

Chapter Ten

THE NEXT DAY, Wednesday, Jeremy was the first one to arrive at the meeting room in the Bison County Government Center. He took the same chair at the round table as the previous week. He removed his briefcase and set it on the table and his backpack on the floor. Then he remembered his water and took it out of his backpack, unscrewed the top, had a sip, and set next to his briefcase. *There*, he thought to himself, *I'm all set.*

He glanced out the window and spent a moment enjoying the peaceful scene outside with the blue sky, white puffy clouds and people strolling by in the sunshine. He cracked a nervous smile, thinking what a nice day it was. *Maybe this will all turn out okay*, he thought to himself. *Maybe after this meeting Ebar will now and forever be known as Kyle, a nice guy who just had a psychotic episode when he was stuck in jail, and life will go on. I'll be his counselor and treat him. He'll get better and will be released and go back to work, and I'll go on to more clients, um, patients, and I'll have a wonderful career. Wouldn't that be nice?*

Pounding footsteps out in the hall destroyed Jeremy's peaceful revery, and moments later, like a herd of charging elephants, Andrews stormed into the room followed closely by Wallace and Kucinen.

"Okay, let's get this show on the road," Andrews instructed, pulling out a chair and sat down, right next to Jeremy who noticed his boss was empty handed except for a mug of tea. Andrews didn't even have a notebook. He glanced at this watch. "It's ten o'clock. Let's go, go, go." He slapped the table hard with each 'go'. Jeremy couldn't help himself; he flinched each time. Wallace and Kucinen noticed and both grinned at his discomfort.

"Shouldn't we wait for Julie?" Jeremy asked, taking a nervous sip of water, trying to collect himself.

"No. It's her fault she's late," Andrews said. "I'll deal with her when it comes time for her performance evaluation." He grinned maliciously and rubbed his hands together like he couldn't wait to take the lone woman in the group down a notch or two.

Then he pointed a finger at Jeremy who by now had been thrown completely off stride by Andrews's aggressive behavior, and said, "Okay, you're on hot-shot. What do have for us?"

Jeremy felt sweat bead up on his forehead, and he fought and urge to wipe it. *Come on, get it together.* He took a breath to settle himself, and then focused on his file for Ebar. Um, Kyle.

"Okay," he said, clearing his throat and trying to sound authoritative. "We're here to talk about my client, Kyle Johnson."

"Stop right there," Andrews interrupted.

Jeremy did as he was told and looked at his boss. "What's up? I thought you wanted to hear about my client?"

"I've been thinking about that," Andrews said, looking smug. "I'll bet you're going to give me some sob-story that he's really okay, just a little rattled."

"Well..." Jeremy stammered.

"And that he's not an alien, he's just confused."

"Actually, yes, I was going to..."

"And that he was under duress at his job and lashed at his co-worker"

"Al. His co-worker's name is..."

Andrews flapped a hand. "Whatever. Al. Schmal. Val. The point is your client attacked him and almost killed him."

"That's right, but..."

"Let me continue." Andrews' eyes shot menacing lasers at Jeremy, making him shut up. "Your client almost killed this Al character and got sent to jail, which he didn't like."

Andrews turned to Wallace and Kucinen and said, "No one would, by the way. Right?"

On cue they both laughed.

"Right on, boss," Wallace said.

"Exactly." Kucinen added.

Andrews continued. "So, your client decides to play the mental health card. He pretends he's crazy and goes into a corner and fakes a call to some imaginary commander in some made-up galaxy far, far away." More laughs from Wallace and Kucinen. "And the jailer hears him, conveniently for Mr. Johnson, by the way, and next thing you know, your client gets sent to the psych ward for evaluation, where he meets you, and you get him sent over there." Andrews stopped talking and pointed in an arbitrary direction indicating the Ryerson Group Home. Wallace and Kucinen both turned to look. Andrews' eyes bored into Jeremy's.

Jeremy made himself look right back at his boss. "Yes, that's sort of what I was going to say, and..."

"Hold on." Andrews commanded, holding up his hand, his steely eyes glaring. He leaned forward so his face was only a couple of feet from Jeremy's. "What I just said. Was that about right or not?"

The last thing he expected was that Andrews was going to take over the meeting, but he had. Jeremey hadn't even had a chance to speak, but he could now. "Well," he stammered, "Here's the deal..."

Andrews had that smirk on his face again, the same one from last week that said he was better than everyone. Especially Jeremy. Andrews sat back, sipped his tea, and dared the young counselor to contradict him. "What's the deal, Mr. Slater? Why don't you tell us exactly what the deal is? Huh?"

Just then Julie rushed into the room. "Sorry I'm late," she said. "What'd I miss?"

Her presence revived Jeremy's good will and intention. He turned to her. "I was just going to tell the group here why I think Eb...I mean Kyle, should be kept in treatment, and not sent back to jail."

"Great," she said, setting her briefcase on the table, pulling up a chair and sitting down across from Jeremy. "Tell me more."

He smiled, feeling a sense of relief, at least for a moment. Julie's presence had shut Andrews up, and he took the opportunity to lay out his plan. "Ebar kept a kind of diary he called his communiques." Jeremy didn't mention that he sent them to commander Zenon on plant Rykos. Why complicate things? "If we could just focus on the incident at the treatment plant for a minute, it's very clear that the employee giving Kyle such a hard time, Al, had it coming to him. I think that Kyle was under a lot of pressure because the city of Orchard Lake was being scrutinized by the MPCA and the MWC and could possibly be sued or at least fined a significant amount of money. He was doing a great job getting a solid testing program up and running, and his boss, Lou, liked him. In fact, Lou said that he'd be willing to vouch for Kyle's character. But then that idiot Al pushed things too far."

Jeremy then told the group about how Kyle had been trapped by Al in the sewer pipe, almost drowned and was barely able to escape with his life. Then he gave a short recap of the fight, pointing out that at the end Kyle had a change of heart and actually saved Al, the man who had tried to kill him.

When he was done, Jeremy summarized and said, "No wonder Kyle went off on Al. The guy shut that grate and trapped him in the pipe. If he hadn't been resourceful and figured out a way to escape, he would have drowned for sure. Al could have claimed he wasn't even in the vicinity of the pipe. He'd be let off Scot free."

Julie spoke up. "I think what Kyle did was justified. Seriously, anyone would have freaked out being trapped like that. Al's lucky Kyle stopped beating him up. In fact, to Kyle's credit, he ended up saving the guy who tried to kill him. There's something good to be said for that."

Jeremy immediately added, "That's right! That very act shows Kyle is a responsible person. It was a very humane response of his, to realize he'd overreacted and then try to do something about it. Which he did. He saved Al."

"I agree," Julie said. She looked around the room, happy she had everyone's attention. "Look, without a doubt I think Kyle needs some more counseling to get his head back together. It's sure to take some time, and I believe Jeremy is the right person for that." She turned to him and asked, "You've established as good bond with him, right? Good rapport?"

Jeremy nodded his head. "I have. We get on really well." He knew exactly what his friend was doing. She was helping to build the case for him to keep treating Kyle (Ebar), and as far as he was concerned, she was doing a great job.

Andrews had been listening to the exchange with a smug expression. He knew Julie and Jeremy were friends. And he knew she was trying to tilt the scale toward trying to improve the client Kyle's mental health instead of sending him back to jail. Which might have been all well and good, except for Andrew's conversation the week before with his friend Jorgenson. It would do neither of them any good if Kyle continued to be an ordinary, run of the mill mental patient who was only stressed out and needed time to get his head back together. No, that wouldn't do at all.

Andrews decided to get to the heart of the matter. "What about all that talk last week about Kyle being an alien? How's that all fit into what you're proposing to do for him?"

Jeremy turned red. "Well, I've thought about it, and it just doesn't seem plausible." He laughed a little hoping it might ease the tension and help prove his point. "I mean, after all, an alien? Like you said, sir, last week," Jeremy leveled his eyes with Andrews, "that's pretty far-fetched." He paused for a moment to let his words sink in, and then added, "Wouldn't you agree?"

That's weird, Andrews thought to himself. *The kid is changing his tune. Well, that's too bad. Time to lower the boom.* "No, I wouldn't agree," he said. He pointed at Wallace and Kucinen and said, "Me and those two have talked about it, and we think there's a very real possibility that Kyle really is an alien."

Jeremy gasped, "Oh, no, sir! That can't be right. He's just slightly misguided." Jeremy felt sweat running down his back. He looked at Julie. Her eyes went wide, and she mouthed, 'Oh, my, god.' Then she said to Jeremy, "You haven't found any real evidence that Kyle's an alien, have you?"

Except for a foot tall stack of communiques written to another alien in another planet in another galaxy far, far away? Jeremy thought factiously.

"Nope. I haven't found a thing," he said, trying to sound as convincing as he could.

Andrews was now in a pickle. He needed Kyle to be an alien. He needed it for his career, and he needed it because Jorgenson at NASA was depending on him. So, he did the only thing he could think do. He said, "Too, bad. I think that there's a very real possibility he is an alien. And as long as I think that he's an alien, he's going to be treated as one." He sat back and raised his voice. "In fact, I've got an announcement to make. I'm going to take over his treatment." He looked at Jeremy. "You've off the case, Slater. Kyle is my responsibility now." His smug smile returned. "Bring me your client's file tomorrow morning. Thursday. We'll meet at the group home." He made it a point of looking at his watch. "I'll see you there at nine." Then he looked around the room and got to his feet. "Meeting adjourned." He pointed at Wallace and Kucinen. "You two. Come with me. I want to bounce some ideas off you both." Then he was gone, Wallace and Kucinen following close behind.

Stunned at the rapid change of events, Jeremy watched the three of them troop out of the room together, grinning and whispering among themselves like the best of buddies. After they left, he turned to Julie and said, "Well, that didn't go too good. Not at all like I'd planned, anyway."

"No kidding," Julie said, shaking her head as their laughter receded down the hall. "There's something weird going on there. I wish I knew what it was." Then, she moved over so she was sitting in the chair next to him and asked, "What are you going to do?"

"I haven't a clue. To be honest, I'm a little rattled." He tossed his empty water bottle in his backpack along with his briefcase. "How about if we go get coffee and talk?"

"Sounds good to me."

***

Later that day, after Andrews had met with Wallace and Kucinen, he called Phil Jorgenson, who answered right away. "What's up? How'd it go?"

"Great. I'm taking over the case of Kyle Johnson."

"What about the case worker? That Jeremy guy?"

"Gone. I booted him. I've got the case now"

"Congratulations," he said.

"Thanks. Give me a week or two with him. I'll get him to believe I'm on his side, and that's it's all to the good that I treat him as an alien. I'll tell him that the publicity will do him wonders. He'll make a lot of friends. Stuff like that. I'll bet he's kind of lonely."

"Brilliant, Rich. Sounds like a good plan to me." Then he paused. "You expect any trouble from Slater?"

Andrews shook his head even though Jorgenson couldn't see it. "Not a bit. The guy's unbelievably passive. Not to mention naïve."

"So… no issues? What about that Julie? Aren't she and Slater friends?"

"If you're implying, 'Are they an item?' the answer is no."

"No? You sure?"

"Absolutely. She a lesbo from the word go. Nothing to worry about from her."

"Good to hear. So, you're all set?"

"Yep. I get the file tomorrow morning, and then he's all mine."

"Congratulations, Rich. This will make you famous."

Andrews chuckled. "I know. You, too."

Jorgenson laughed. "I'm looking forward to it.

Chapter Eleven

JEREMY AND JULIE walked down the street to the Bison Café, the same one they'd gone to the week before. They ordered coffee at the counter, and then sat at a front window table where Jeremy nervously started playing with a paper napkin. He was new to the world of counseling, having only been onboard for about a month and a half. Whatever he'd expected as an outcome of the meeting they'd just attended, it wasn't what had happened.

"Man, what was the deal back there?" he finally said, pointing back toward the government building. He set down his shredded napkin and picked up his mug. "That did not go well." He took a sip. "Yikes. That's hot!"

At eleven in the morning the café was nearly empty. It was the third week in September, and the sunshine, blue sky and warm weather should have made him feel on top of the world. Or at least happy. But, no, none of that mattered. What mattered was that he had lost Ebar.

Julie added some cream to her mug and stirred it in. "There's something weird going on with Andrews," she said, taking a sip. "That wasn't like at all like him to take over your case like he did. In fact, it's my opinion that he really doesn't like counseling our patients all that much. They're just a means to an end for him."

"A means to an end? What do you mean by that?"

"Advancing his career."

"Oh." Jeremy was quiet for a moment digesting her words. Finally, he spat out, "What a jerk."

Julie raised her mug in acknowledgment. "My sentiments exactly." She took a sip. "I've never liked him."

Jeremy picked up another napkin and started to tear into it. Julie put her hand on his. "Hey, take it easy there, my friend. Give that poor napkin a break."

"Sorry," he grinned sheepishly. He set the napkin down and let out a long sigh. "I guess I'm at my wits end. I have no idea what I'm going to do."

"How do you think Ebar's going to respond?"

Jeremy shook his head sadly. "That's a good question. I'd like to think he's going to miss me. We had a good bond going. A good connection."

"Yeah, you did. But now he gets what he wants. Now he gets to be a real alien."

"There's something strange about Andrews wanting to do that, don't you think?"

"I do. He was so adamant against Ebar and his being an alien last week. Now..."

"Now a big change." Jeremy looked at Julie, put out his hand and turned it over. "A one-hundred- and eighty-degrees flip-flop." He took a sip of his coffee. "I hate to say this, because I always try to look at the good side of people, but I'm not sure I trust him."

Julie smiled. Jeremy's naiveté was sweet, but dangerous, a sure recipe for disappointment in the real world they dealt with. But sweet, nonetheless. "Well, join the club. I've known him since he's been here, for ten years, and I can tell you this: I don't trust him at all. He's just out to make a name for himself. He doesn't care about anyone but Doctor Richard Andrews. I think your patient Ebar is in for a rude awakening. It's not going to be all peaches and cream for him."

"I was thinking the same thing."

They were silent for a minute, thinking and looking out the window. Jeremy loved the out of doors. He enjoyed birdwatching and hiking and right now he'd give anything to be doing either one of them. Or both. But he shook those kinds of thoughts from his brain. He needed to focus. His gut told him Ebar might be in trouble.

Julie said, "What do you think Ebar really wants?"

"I know exactly what he wants. He's lost touch with Commander Zenon, and he's upset by that. He wants to get

113

back in contact with him."

"Then what?"

"I'm not sure."

"You're not?"

"No. I think he's tired of being a spy for the commander. I think he wants to go home. I think he likes earth and a lot of people he's met, but I think he's tired, and mentally fatigued. I really think he just wants to leave."

"What about that mission? You know, to study earth and make a recommendation to this Zenon guy about whether or not they should take us over?" She looked Jeremy straight in the eyes. "In my mind that's a pretty big deal." Jeremy smiled, and Julie said, "What's so funny? I don't think getting taken over by a warlord freak from another solar system is any laughing matter. Not at all."

"Oh, I'm not laughing," Jeremy said, composing himself.

"What then?"

"You're talking like you believe he really is a real alien."

"Oh." Julie sat back and was quiet for a moment, thinking about what Jeremy had just said. She hadn't known him long, but she'd known him long enough to trust his instincts. He was a pretty perceptive guy, at least from what she'd seen anyway. She took a sip of coffee, sat forward and locked eyes with him and said, "You know what? Maybe I do."

"Welcome aboard," Jeremy said, grinning for real, now. In spite of the dire situation, it was good to know she was on his side.

"So, what are you going to do?"

"I'm going to talk to Ebar. We've got to get somethings ironed out. Want to come?"

"Yes. I sure do."

Jeremy finished his coffee and grabbed his backpack. "Then, let's go."

Julie picked up her briefcase. "I'm right with you."

***

While Jeremy and Julie were talking in the coffee shop and planning their next move, Ebar had just finished a group counseling session. On the way back to his room, he had let himself fall behind, and then ducked into the mechanical room for the home. It was a noisy, cramped space full of dust and cobwebs, but that was okay. Behind the furnace was enough space for him to pull up a metal stool. He sat down facing the corner and closed his eyes. He took a minute to control his breathing, clear his mind and shut down his senses. Soon, he had reached such a deep meditative state that he didn't even hear the air-conditioning equipment running. He had become one with his mind.

He sent out his thoughts to Zenon: *Commander. Commander are you there?*

Nothing.

Forcing himself to stay calm, he again sent out his thoughts. *Commander Zenon, I need to talk to you.*

Again, nothing.

Ebar was about ready to give up when all of a sudden, a transmission came back to him. *Ebar. Ebar, is that you?*

Ebar's heart raced. It was Commander Zenon! Ebar breathed deeply to settle himself. *Yes, Commander. It is me, Ebar.*

Finally, Zenon said. *I've been trying to reach you.*

Dispensing with any pleasantries, as much as he'd like to just talk, Ebar said, *What is it? What's going on?*

The water supply here on Rykos is critically low. We are in need of moving to another planet. I require your assessment of earth. Soon.

Ebar was shocked. As much as he knew that this was the purpose of his mission and that this day would eventually come, he wasn't prepared for it to be right now. *Um, I can certainly do that, sir.*

Good. I want a report. I want it thorough. It will help me decide whether to come to earth and begin our takeover. Or not. I have a few other planets I'm considering.

I will do that, sir. If I may ask, when you will contact me?

One week from today. Maybe sooner.

Okay, then. Understood.

And Ebar?

Yes, sir?

Don't try to get a hold of me. I will get in touch with you.

And with that, the transmission ended. Zenon was gone.

Ebar came out of his trance-like state, opened his eyes, and stared into the concrete corner of the mechanical room, thinking, *well, that was an odd conversation*. He hadn't talked to Zenon in months and now all of a sudden, he was being called upon to make an assessment of earth. Should he recommend take-over or not? Take-over was Zenon's way of saying, 'We will bring total annihilation. We will kill everyone on earth and replace the humans with citizens from Rykos.' Zenon had done it before with a few other planets, and he wouldn't hesitate to do it again with earth. All he needed was Ebar's say so, and Zenon would attack.

Unsure what he was going to do, Ebar was headed back to his room when one of the orderlies stopped him.

"Kyle, where were you? We were looking for you."

"Oh, hi. Sorry about that. I had to use the restroom really bad. I apologize."

The orderly looked closely his patient. *Was Kyle lying?* Ebar cracked a smile, and the orderly automatically smiled back, shrugging off his concern. Kyle was pretty harmless. "Okay. That's fine. Are you sure you're all right?"

Ebar nodded, "Yes, I am. I'm good. Thank you for asking."

"Okay. I just wanted to tell you that your shrink, Jeremy called. He said he was on his way over to talk to you. I guess he's bringing someone called Julie."

"Okay. Great. Thank you."

Ebar hurried back to his room, thinking, *so Jeremy and Julie are coming by. I wonder what that's all about? It's probably got something to do with that meeting with Andrews*. The more he thought about it, the more thought, *yeah, that's got to be it*.

He didn't know whether to happy or sad.

Or afraid.

Chapter Twelve

WHEN JEREMY AND Julie showed up, Ebar was a nervous wreck. He had decided to come clean, and before the two of them had barely stepped into his room, he told them about being in contact with Zenon. That had generated a lively discussion.

Jeremy wanted to know the logistics. "Where'd it happen?" he asked, and when told that it'd been in the mechanical room, all he could say was, "Huh. Imagine that."

Julie was more pragmatic. "What'd you guys talk about?" That's when it got interesting.

"Zenon's thinking about taking over earth."

"What!" Jeremy and Julie both shouted simultaneously.

"Quiet," Ebar pointed to the hall and put his finger to his lip to admonish them. "But, yeah, it's pretty crazy."

To say Jeremy and Julie were concerned was putting it mildly.

"You better start at the beginning," Jeremy said, lowering his voice to a whisper. "So, you made contact with Zenon, right?"

"Right."

"And then he told you about taking over earth for its water supply. Correct?"

"Correct."

Jeremy shook his head. "Why would he do that?"

"We've had a shortage for nearly one-hundred years," Ebar said. "The scientists have been working on various processes to make water, but none of them have been successful. At least that was Zenon told me. So, plan B has always been to take over another planet and use its water supply. Yours has always been up there at the top of the list."

"You mean there were others?" Julie asked.

Jeremy and Julie looked at each other, both thinking, *well, that answers the question about other life in the universe.* Jeremy spoke up, "What's this takeover going to look like?"

Ebar's face turned red. "I'm embarrassed to say," he

stammered, "that it won't be pretty. The scientists have developed high power beams of light, sort of like your lasers, that they will use to essentially vaporize all life on earth. Then our spaceships will come and the process of repopulating your planet will begin with men, women, and children, along with our own plants and animals, even insects. Commander Zenon has overseen doing this with other planets. It's all very well planned and thought out." He paused and looked sadly at the two of them. He had developed a fondness for Jeremy and was developing an affection for Julie as well. They were both nice people. It too bad they had would have to die.

Or did they?

Ebar took off his glasses, polished them with is handkerchief and said, "You know, there might be a way out of this."

"What?" Jeremy asked. His mind was racing. Aliens taking over earth. Mass annihilation. It was all too much. He glanced at Julie who was doing something on her phone.

Ebar put his glasses back on. "Zenon gave me a week to pull together my notes so I can present to him what I've found since I've been here."

"So, you're saying that it's not a done deal, Zenon attacking earth?"

"Correct. I'm saying that maybe I can make earth look like it's not the prime takeover candidate that I've been saying it is."

Jeremy's eyes went wide. "You can do that?"

Ebar looked at him seriously. "I can try. Zenon is very

adamant about earth, but I think I can make the case for not coming here for the water."

"How so?"

"Leave it to me. But it has to do with pollution and global warming."

"Well, if you think…"

Julie spoke up. "Sorry to interrupt, Jeremy, we've got another issue to deal with. Remember Andrews?" She looked at Ebar. "Andrews wants to take over your case from Jeremy. He's going to present you to the world as an alien."

Ebar cracked a wide smile at the potentially good news for him. "Really? That's great!"

Julie held up a hand. "Stop right there. It's not that great, Ebar, not at all. Andrews is not like Jeremy here who is not only a nice guy, but someone who is definitely looking out for your best interests." Jeremy blushed. "Andrews is a jerk. HHe'll keep you under lock and key with the pretense of studying you and protecting you or some such nonsense, and you'll never have a moment's peace and quiet. And time to yourself? Forget about it. You'll be monitored every second of your life." She paused and then asked, "How's that sound to you?"

Ebar was aghast. "Not good at all!" Sweat beaded up on his forehead, and his knees went weak. He fell back to sitting on his bed, clutching his water bottle like a security blanket. He looked frantically to Jeremy and Julie. "Can you guys help me?"

Julie looked at Jeremy and winked. Then she said to Ebar, "I think so. I'm starting to work out a plan."

"What is it?" Jeremy and Ebar both asked at the same time.

Julie grinned. "It involves my partner Wren and our RV. I was just texting her."

"I was wondering about that," Jeremy said.

"What's an RV?" Ebar asked.

Jeremy answered, "It's a recreational vehicle. Remember last week when I told you about Julie and Wren and their vacation?"

"Oh, yeah, right," Ebar said, and took a sip of his water. Ever polite he said, "Your vacation sounded like fun."

Julie smiled. "Well, it would have been, but that's on hold for the moment because what's going right now is a very big deal, Ebar, with you and Zenon, and you and Andrews. I think we need to get away from here for a while. At least get away from that creep Andrews. I told Wren about what was going on, and she suggested something, and I agree with her. How about if we use my RV and hit the road?"

"Hit the road?" Jeremy said. "Why?"

"Because I don't trust Andrews. He's going to essentially hold Ebar prisoner for the rest of his life. You don't want that, do you?"

"Of course not!"

She looked at Ebar and didn't even have to ask the question. He shook his head to the negative. "No!"

"Good," she said. "So, we're all agreed. We're going to get out of here. Oh, and one other thing."

"What's that?" Jeremey asked.

"She wants to come with."

"Really?" Jeremy said. "Does she know what she's in for?"

"You bet she does. In fact, she was the one who suggested we take the RV."

"Wow," Ebar said. "She sounds awesome."

Julie smiled. "She is."

They talked a little longer and then Julie stood up. "Okay you guys, I'm going to get going. I've got to talk more with Wren and work out the details." She looked at the two of them. "Like where we're going to go. Obviously. That's a pretty big deal. But, no matter what, I want to make sure we've got enough supplies. Remember, Wren and I were going to leave on our vacation on Friday anyway, so no one should suspect anything weird on our part if the RV is gone a day early."

"You sure she's all right with this?" Jeremy asked. He'd only known Julie since he'd started working for the county. They'd gotten along great right from the start, and Julie had always talked about Jeremy coming over for dinner, but that hadn't happened. Now, they'd be traveling together. "We must be breaking some kind of law, or something, right?"

Julie smiled at Jeremy, and then looked at Ebar. "Are you okay going on the run with me and Wren and Jeremy? At least until we figure out our next step?"

Ebar answered immediately, "Yes, absolutely! Especially, if the alternative is waiting around until tomorrow and putting my life in the hands of Doctor Richard Andrews. The guy sounds like a real piece of work."

Julie squeezed Ebar's arm in a show of affection. "Oh, I'm sure he has his good points. I just don't know what they are."

In spite of the tension situation, they all laughed.

Julie looked at Jeremy. "You're going to have to figure out a way to get Ebar out of here without arousing suspicion. The longer we can keep what we're doing a secret from Andrews, the better off we'll be."

"I know. I'm working on an idea." He looked at Ebar who was watching the conversation closely. "I think it'll work. I'm going to stay here for a while and talk to Ebar about it. Call me when you've talked to Wren. Okay?"

"Okay." Julie gave Jeremy and Ebar each a quick hug. "Talk to you soon."

***

After Julie left, Jeremy said to Ebar, "We've got to talk." He sat on the desk chair and Ebar on the bed. "What do you think about all of this?" Jeremy waved his hand around in a circle. "It might seem like a little too much for you. Is it?"

Ebar sat forward and said, "Look, I know it's sudden, but I'm okay with that. From where I'm coming from, two months ago I was working a pretty mellow job at the treatment plant. My biggest worry was not hearing form Zenon. Then Al started hassling me, I lost my temper, almost killed him, and ended up in jail. Then I made a mistake of trying to talk to Zenon and the jailer heard me and reported me. Then I was sent to the psych ward for evaluation and shot up with drugs to calm me down and then you showed up." Ebar paused, looked at Jeremy and smiles. "Thankfully."

Jeremy turned red. "You don't need to say that but thank you."

Ebar continued. "So, you showed up and took over my case, and we talked and got to know each other." He stopped again and took a deep breath. "And you came to believe me about being an alien. Which is very cool. Which I really appreciate." He stopped again and said, "And I hope this doesn't sound too weird, but I'll say it anyway. I think of you as a friend. The only friend I've ever had on earth. And that means a lot to me." With that he got up, and went to Jeremy said, "And I thank you for that." And then he shook Jeremy's hand.

Jeremy was stunned, but in a good way. "So, you're okay escaping with me and Julie and Wren?"

"Yes," Ebar said. Of course.

Jeremy grinned. "Good. Because I think it's our best option. Look I've only been at this job six weeks, hardly anytime at all. But I do know this - there's something off about Andrews. I like you and respect your desire to live as an alien, and I want to help you with that. For now, hitting the road is our best option."

Ebar sat back down on his bed. He'd never felt so good. "You think this will work? Can we elude Andrews?"

"I think we'll do everything in our power to keep you free. How's that sound?"

126

"That sounds great."

Okay, here's what I'm thinking...

Chapter Thirteen

IT WAS JEREMY who came up with the plan to fake going to the Mayo Clinic. It was Wren who came up with the idea to go north to Lake Superior.

After Julie texted Wren from Ebar's room and briefly explained the situation with Andrews wanting to take over Ebar's case, Wren didn't have to think. She'd texted back, "You want to help them, right?"

"Yeah, I do. I like Jeremy, and it's not every day you get to do something nice for an alien."

Wren had grinned to herself. It was one of the many things she loved about her partner. She was such a kind person. An idea came to her immediately. She texted back, "I'm all for it. I'm thinking maybe we should take the RV."

"Taking the RV sounds like a great idea. I'll be home soon. We can talk over the details then."

When she returned from the group home, Julie went downstairs to where Wren had her office and studio. After she got done explaining the situation with Jeremy and Ebar, she sat down next to Wren's desk and said, "I was thinking we could take them with us out west in the RV. It's a good place to get lost in out there. Lots of wide-open spaces. We could go off the grid for a while and figure out what to do."

"Your idiot boss knows where we're going, right? Yellowstone?"

"Yeah, I had to request vacation time a month ago. It's policy."

"Do you think he might suspect you're helping Jeremy? I mean he'll probably figure out something is up pretty quick."

"Probably," Julie said, thoughtfully. "He's going to go to the group home tomorrow morning to talk to Ebar."

"So that doesn't give us much time."

"But we might have more time that we think. Jeremy's going to get him away from there somehow. He's going to call me later with the details."

Wren grinned. "Good. That'll be interesting. From what you've told me, he's a straight arrow kind of a guy. I'm curious as to what he's going to come up with."

130

"Me, too," Julie said, a shadow of concern passing over her face. Had they bit off more than they could chew? She shook her head to the negative. No. They could make this happen. She collected herself and continued, "So Ebar is covered for tonight and into tomorrow. But we can assume that by sometime tomorrow Andrews will figure out that Jeremy's kidnapped our alien."

"Our alien?" Wren asked, grinning. "That sounds a little possessive, don't you think?"

"I only mean it in a good way," Julie smiled. "Like we care about him."

"Just kidding, lover."

Julie laughed. "I hear you, though. I *do* care about him. He's a good guy. Trusting. But a little naïve, I think."

Wren sat back, thinking out loud, and said, "You know, this could be a good thing, though, for Ebar. Get him away from Ryerson for a while and the group home."

"And the hospital. And the police station."

"Right. Give him a chance to regroup."

"Speaking of regrouping, there's something else you should know about," Julie said, shifting closer and taking Wren's hand. "It's pretty incredible."

Wren leaned forward. She knew by the tone of her voice that Julie was deadly serious. "Ebar has been in touch with his home planet and his commander."

"Really?"

"Yes. Let me fill you in." Julie briefly told Wren about Zenon and the lack of water on Rykos and the possible takeover of earth and the annihilation of all living things.

131

Just putting it into words made the whole thing seems unbelievable. Unreal. Like something out of a science fiction movie. "So, there's a lot going on."

All things considered; Wren took the news well. "All the more reason to get away. Without a doubt Ebar will need to focus and concentrate," Wren said. "And, hopefully, do the right thing when he communicates with this Zenon guy again."

"Yeah, my thought exactly."

"Well, in that case, I think we shouldn't go west. It's a lot of driving, for one thing. Plus, it's the first place Andrews would have the authorities look for us if they followed up on employees that know Jeremy. People know you and he are close, right?"

"Right."

Wren pondered for a moment, and then said, "So, let's do something different. I'm going to assume Andrews will file a missing person's report when he can't find Ebar. The cops will then get involved."

"Yeah, I know. I'm not sure Jeremy's thought through all of that."

"So, we'll do some thinking for him. I'm wondering if maybe we should take them up the north shore."

"Lake Superior?"

"Yeah, there are plenty of campgrounds there. We should be able to find a spot. It's Wednesday now and Thursday tomorrow. They don't usually start filling up until Friday."

"That's a great idea. Plus, there's something else, too, that makes the north shore a good choice."

"What's that?"

"Ebar loves water. It's like an emotional thing for him. Something to do with him and his mother and a reservoir on his home planet."

Wren smiled. "Well, there you go. Lake Superior it is."

"I'll call Jeremy."

Wren checked the time. "It's three o'clock. Tell him we'll pick him up at that coffee shop you and he go to at six. That'll give us plenty of time to finish packing."

"I'm on it." Julie took out her phone, but before she made the call, she said, "Thanks for all this, Wren. I really appreciate it."

"Don't mention it," Wren grinned. She stood up and hugged Julie. "This'll be fun."

***

Jeremy was talking with Ebar in his room when Julie's call came through. He answered, "Hi Julie, what's up?"

She told him about the plan Wren had come up with. When she finished, she asked "What do you think?"

Jeremy was nervous, but also committed to saving Ebar from Andrews. "Sounds good to me." He looked at Ebar, who was watching the conversation intently. "Plus, it entails water so I'm sure Ebar will love it."

"Good. I'll let you guys get back to doing whatever you were doing."

133

"I'm telling Ebar about the plan I came up with to get him out of here."

"What is it?"

"I'm going to talk to the house manager here, Clara Simpson, and fake that we have to go for psychiatric tests at the Mayo Clinic in Rochester. I'll tell her that we have to stay overnight, because Ebar is supposed to be monitored at the psychiatric ward there. I'll tell her I'm going to rent a motel room and stay overnight, pick Ebar up in the morning and that we'll be home tomorrow by noon."

"Wow, that's pretty ingenious. What's Ebar think?"

"Oh, you know Ebar," he said, smiling at his friend who smiled back. "He's pretty agreeable."

"Okay. Well, it sounds good to me. I'll see you at the coffee shop in town in three hours."

After they hung up, Jeremy looked at Ebar. "Okay, Julie and Wren have a plan."

"I heard you mention water."

"Right. I'll tell you about in a minute, but first I want to know if you're good with our idea to get you out of here."

"Boy am I ever. Think Ms. Simpson will buy it?"

"Yes. I've got a good rapport with her. Andrews is another matter. He's supposed to come for you tomorrow morning, and when he finds you're not here he'll blow a gasket."

"But we'll be long gone by then, right?"

"Right," Jeremy said. "On the road."

Ebar suddenly became nervous. "Are you expecting

trouble?"

"Hey, don't worry about it. We've got you covered." Ebar relaxed and took a sip of water.

"Okay. I'm not worried if you aren't."

As Jeremy watched Ebar drink, his throat suddenly went dry. Not because of thirst, but because the magnitude of what they were doing suddenly hit him. They were actually going to kidnap Ebar and go on the run. He had no idea how many laws they'd be breaking, but he bet it was a lot. He watched as Ebar put the cap on his water bottle, and then look out the window to the sunny day beyond. Jeremy smiled. His alien friend was such a nice guy. Helping him was the right thing to do. He was sure of it.

Jeremy cleared his throat to get Ebar's attention. "We'll take good care of you." He smiled what he hoped was a confident smile, and then added, "I think you'll love this. We're going to escape to the north shore, up by Lake Superior. It's the biggest freshwater lake in the world. We'll hide out up there until we decide what to do next."

"I've heard about that lake. Gitchigumi is what the native Americans called it. I've always wanted to see it. This'll be great."

In spite of his worries about what they were doing, Jeremy was happy to see Ebar's enthusiasm. He wished he could share in it, but, unfortunately, he couldn't. Not right now, anyway. Instead, he looked out the window, his mind racing. *What we're going to be doing will be a lot of things*, is what he was thinking. *Hopefully, great will be one of them.*

Chapter Fourteen

JEREMY'S CAR WAS a used Honda Civic that had nearly one hundred and fifty thousand miles on it. The old beater had seen better days, but it got him and Ebar to the coffee shop on time, and that was the important thing. Right at six o'clock they pulled into the parking lot next to the RV.

Julie had been watching for them and jumped out. Wren joined her. "Hi Jeremy. Hi Ebar." She turned and said, "And here is my partner, Wren."

Wren shook each of their hands. To her, Jeremy looked

like Julie had described him: a large, teddy bear of a man with a full beard. He was wearing blue jeans, a red flannel shirt and work boots. He looked kind of like the mythical Northwoods legend Paul Bunyan.

Ebar, on the other hand, couldn't have been more different. He was thin, just under six feet tall and dressed in orange running shoes, khaki pants and a blue checked long-sleeved shirt buttoned all the way to the top. His sandy hair and black framed glasses completed his unassuming look.

They each had a backpack, filled, Wren guessed, with their clothes and other essentials.

As she shook their hands, she smiled at them. Wren was a naturally cheerful woman, happy with life, and she was looking forward the challenge that lay ahead. "Great to meet you both," she said, and opened the side door of the RV. "Toss your stuff in there and make yourself comfortable." She looked at Julie and grinned. "We'll ride up in front. I'll take the first shift."

Julie turned to Jeremy and Ebar. "Wren likes to be in charge, if you can't tell."

"That's good," Jeremy said, " because I'm still pretty nervous about what we're doing."

Julie said, "I think we're okay for now. No one knows what we've done. As far as Andrews is concerned, Ebar's at the group home and is tucked in for the night. And as far as the group home is concerned, you've taken him to the Mayo Clinic." She checked her watch. "It's just after six. We've got probably until nine tomorrow morning before Andrews figures out something is wrong."

"Then what?" Jeremy asked.

138

Julie looked at Wren who chuckled and said, "As they say, the s-h-i-t will hit the fan. But, by then, we'll be long gone." She checked the side mirrors and concentrated on getting out of the parking lot. The RV was relatively small, about twenty-two feet long, but still required concentration to drive. "For now, let's get this show on the road."

Ebar piped up. "That sounds good to me." He looked at Jeremy. "Don't worry. I have a feeling between you and Julie and Wren, things will work out just fine."

Wren grinned and said, "That's the spirit, Ebar. I like your thinking. In fact, why don't you and Julie switch places. Come up in front and we can chat and get to know each other."

"I'd love to!"

Ebar got settled in the passenger's seat and Wren asked, "Have you ever been to Lake Superior?"

"I've heard of it, but, no, I've never been there."

"Oh, boy, do we have a treat in store for you."

They left Ryerson and drove on little used county roads to the north and east before picking up Interstate 35W just south of Hinkley. Jeremy had only known Julie since he'd been hired and had never met Wren, and Julie and Ebar hardly knew each other, and Wren didn't know either of them, but by the time they pulled into a gas station two hours later in Hinkley to fuel up, they were all talking amiably with one another.

"It's got to be the situation," Julie said, standing next to Wren as she filled the gas tank.

"What do mean?"

They both watched Jeremy and Ebar head into the station to use the restroom. Julie said, "This whole thing is very serious. Jeremy kidnaped Ebar, and we're aiding and abetting them. I'm going to probably lose my job over this."

Wren laughed as she put the nozzle away. "I'd say losing your job is the least of your worries, my dear. You...we could all end up doing jail time."

Wren was going to use her credit card to pay for the gas when Julie stopped her. "Wait."

"What? Why?" Then it dawned on her. "Oh. I see what you mean. They could trace the credit card, right?"

Julie nodded. "Yeah. If they put it together that we're helping them."

"Okay. I've got some cash," Wren said, heading inside to pay. "I'll tell you one thing, though."

"What's that?" Julie asked, walking with her.

"I think our lives are about to change in a big way."

Julie grimaced as she nodded to the affirmative. "No kidding." She looked at Wren. "You still up for this?"

Wren reached over and kissed the top of Julie's head. "Wouldn't miss it for the world, babe."

A little while later, they were all situated back in the RV with Julie taking Ebar's place in the passenger's seat. Wren continued driving and in the back seat Ebar opened a plastic bag. "Here you go," he said, and handed out bottled water to everyone. "I don't what it is, but I've been really thirsty lately."

"Thanks," Julie said, unscrewing the cap and taking a drink. She turned to Jeremy. "You've been awfully quiet. I know there's a million things on your mind. What are you thinking about?"

Jeremy drank from his bottle, then said, "What I'm thinking about is that I really want to thank you and Wren. The more I think about it, the more it's dawning on me that I'm getting you two in a mess of trouble. Me, I don't mind. I'm doing this for Ebar."

Wren kept her eyes on the road, but turned slightly, "Stop it right there, buddy!" she admonished him. "Yeah, you may have acted rashly, but you did the right thing. Andrews was going to screw up Ebar's life and make joke out of him. Lots of people would have given in and let it happen, but you didn't. In my book, that's fantastic."

Jeremy's ears turned red. "You think so?"

"I know so. Right, Julie?"

"Right. I've been doing this for sixteen years. Don't get me wrong, I love what I do, but maybe even I've gotten a little jaded over all that time, especially since Andrews took over. When I heard about Ebar and how you came to believe in him, it did something to me, too."

"What's that?" Jeremy asked.

"It made me realize that if we could just help Ebar - help him get his feet on the ground, and maybe even help him deal with this Zenon fellow, it'd all be worth it. And you know why?"

"Why?"

"Because, like Wren said, it's the right thing to do."

Out of the blue Ebar reached into the front seat and gave Julie a hug. "Thank you," he said.

She hugged him back. "No. Thank you."

Jeremy watched the two of them the hugging, and, suddenly, he felt a slight sense of relief. "So, it's okay, I take it, that you guys are helping us?" he asked, joking a little, after Ebar sat back down beside him.

Wren whooped from the driver's seat, "Hell, yes! Of course, it's okay. In fact, Ebar, if you're passing out hugs, lean over here and give me one. I could use it."

Happily, he did. Without thinking twice.

Chapter Fifteen

THEY MADE IT to Duluth around ten o'clock that night, coming into town down a high bluff which overlooked the city before winding back and forth on a steep grade toward the downtown district and Lake Superior. Wren pumped the breaks all the way to slow the heavy RV. The sun had been set for over an hour, and the bright city lights lit up the night sky. Ebar, however, ignored it all. Instead, he was glued to the window, blown away by the expanse of the huge body of water that lay before them disappearing into inky darkness. He said it well when he pointed out, after being speechless for a few minutes, "It's like staring into the void of the universe."

The three other nodded whole-heartedly in agreement.

Wren drove through town while Julie spread open a map of Minnesota on her knees and consulted it.

"We should keep going north on Highway 61," she said. "There are campgrounds all along the way from here to Canada."

"Sounds good," Wren said, sipping from a container of coffee. They'd stopped at a rest stop a half hour outside of Duluth to stretch their legs and get some beverages which ended up being black coffee for everyone except for Ebar who stuck with his every present bottle of water.

In the middle of downtown, when they came to a stoplight, near the famous former brewery *Fitgers*, now a swank hotel, Julie turned to Jeremy and Ebar and asked, "Are you guys doing okay back there?"

Ebar spoke up. "I'm doing great." He pointed to his right where Lake Superior was less than a block away. "This is amazing. I've never seen a lake so big before."

Wren laughed, "What until you see it in the morning."

"I can't wait," he said, almost gleefully. Then he pointed again. "Hey, I see some lights way out there. What are they, do you suppose?"

Jeremy said, "Those are big iron ore boats. Or ships, I guess they call them. They dock in Duluth and the town next to it, Superior, Wisconsin, and drop off their loads and pick up other cargo. It's a big deal for both cities. Brings in a lot of commerce."

144

Julie looked at him. "Look at you, mister know-it-all," she joked. "I'm impressed."

Jeremy blushed. "My parents took me and my little brother here once about ten years ago. It was fun."

"So, we'll have those ships with us as company?" Ebar asked. "I like that." Then he yawned. "Sorry. Long day."

Jeremy said, thinking back to the meeting that morning which had been the start of the journey they were now on, "Don't worry about it. It's been a long day for all of us."

"That's true," Ebar said. He leaned forward and put his hand on both Julie and Wren's shoulders. "I don't want to sound like a broken record, but I have tell you again how thankful I am you guys are doing this. I appreciate it so much."

Julie grinned at him, "Don't worry about it." She patted Ebar's hand and then turned to Wren. "It was time for an adventure, right?"

Wren grinned. "Right. Besides, I haven't been up here since I was a kid. It'll be fun."

As they drove north and left the city, the road turned to two lanes and Wren slowed the RV, driving carefully over the twisting and turning road. Even though it was after Labor Day and the tourist season was officially over, there was still traffic, and she concentrated on driving, lowering her headlight beams when cars approached and slowing down a little when cars from behind passed them. It was slow going, but that was okay. Ebar was sitting close to the window so he could watch the lake, and the ore boats out on the water, now that he knew what they were.

Jeremy hadn't been saying much the entire trip because

he was slowly coming to grips with the fact that by taking Ebar and going on the run, he was essentially changing the course of his life forever. *What are my parents going to think about that?* He wondered. *And Jonny. What about him?*

Jeremy had grown up on a dairy farm in central Minnesota. His father was a full-time farmer, and his mother helped out working long hours with him in addition to taking care of Jonny, Jeremy's younger brother, who had been born with multiple sclerosis. It was her caring nature, and the fact that Jeremy loved his brother and enjoyed helping his mom with him, that led Jeremy to the healthcare profession. He chose mental health because he was interested in people and how their minds worked. The fact that sometimes people needed help was something he wanted to be a part of. He went to college, worked hard and when he got his first job, the job he had now, he'd been overjoyed. So were his parents. So was Jonny. They'd thrown him a big party at the farm and as far as Jeremy was concerned, his life was mapped out for him. He'd be a mental health professional for the rest of his life.

But now this. By taking Ebar, his life would be forever changed. He made a mental note to write his mom a long letter explaining what he was doing and wh. He owed that much to her at least.

To shake his melancholy mood, he looked at Ebar and asked, "How are you doing?"

Ebar pried his eyes away from looking into the black night trying to catch glimpses of the lake and said, "Fine. Great, actually." He smiled. "I can't believe we're really doing this."

"Me neither. Are you sure you're all right being on the

run?

Ebar turned so he was facing Jeremy. "Absolutely. Remember, if you hadn't taken me, I'd be having to deal with Andrews. I don't think that was going to work out to be such a good deal."

"Me neither." Jeremy sighed. "What's done is done, though."

"I know." Ebar smiled and clasped Jeremy on the arm. "Hey, don't worry. You did a good thing. I'm glad you did what you did. Really glad."

"That's good." *Now, if I only knew what to do next.*

Jeremy's thought was interrupted by Julie. "Wren, there's a campground coming up we should check out. I've looked it up on my phone. It's called *Cozy Cove*. The website says there're spaces available."

"Sweet. Sounds good to me."

Wren drove another mile or so until she saw the well-lit sign. It turned out that Cozy Cove was a state park with a campground associated with it. At the entrance there was a drop-box. They stopped and put their license number on an envelope along with money for one overnight stay and put it into the box.

"All set," Wren said, slowly pulling ahead. The headlights cut through the night. The road was gravel and wound through a forest of aspen, oak, and maple trees like a coiled snake.

"This is so cool," Ebar said.

Jeremy smiled. *Just like something my kid brother Jonny would say.*

Julie was looking at a map of the campground on her phone. "It says there are twenty spaces." She watched out her window. "It looks like most of them are empty. That's good."

Ebar asked, "Do you think we can we get close to the lake?"

Julie looked at her phone. "Yeah, we can." She looked up and pointed, "Wren, turn left up there."

Wren did and eased the RV down a narrow one lane road hemmed in by evergreen trees. They all rolled down their windows and the aromatic scent of pine and cedar and juniper filled the interior of the RV.

"Wow, does that ever smell great!" Ebar exclaimed. Then, he said, "Wait a minute, I hear something."

Julie leaned her head out the window. "You do, Ebar. Guess what it is?"

"It sounds like the ocean."

She grinned at him. "It kind of is. It's Lake Superior. Those are waves crashing on the rocks."

"Oh, man. That's fantastic!"

Wren drove forward only another fifty feet or so before pulling into a space to park the RV. "Home sweet home," she said, coasting to a stop. There was a campfire ring of rocks to their right along with a picnic table. She'd barely turned off the engine when Ebar bolted out the door. He stood in the middle of their camping space and breathed deeply, inhaling the pine scented air. Jeremy, Julie, and Wren joined him, and they all stood together under a clear, star-lit night sky.

148

An owl suddenly began hooting as if welcoming them. A light breeze wafted through the trees whispering its own greeting. Nearby the sound of the waves on the rocky shore pounded relentlessly, as if beckoning them.

Ebar looked at his friends and said, "Let's go check out the lake."

His enthusiasm was infectious. "Let's!" Came a chorus of three voices.

Julie used the flashlight function on her phone to lead, with Ebar right on her shoulder and Jeremy and Wren crowding close behind. They followed a pine needle path fifty feet through the forest, the sound of the waves drawing them ever closer. A minute later, they came out of the trees and stood on an overlook about twenty feet above the water.

"Let's keep going," Ebar said.

So, they did, carefully making their way down a narrow, rocky path to the shore. In the bright moonlight, they could see the beach was made of walnut sized rocks, worn smooth by centuries of wind and wave action. In front of them, the lake stretched out into the darkness, and on each side of them, to the right and left, the forest encircled the shoreline forming, like the name of the campground implied, a cozy cove.

"This is incredible," Ebar exclaimed. "I feel like I've come home."

His three friends watched him prancing on the beach, smiling at his obvious joy and happiness, each of them having a variation of the same thought - that no matter what the outcome of this adventure might be, seeing Ebar so happy had just made it all worthwhile.

Chapter Sixteen

DOCTOR RICHARD ANDREWS awoke on Thursday morning feeling on top of the world. *Just think*, he thought to himself, standing in the shower, and humming a country western song he couldn't remember the name of, *I've got my own alien!* He chuckled, getting out, drying himself off and admiring himself in the full-length mirror. Tan and fit after a summer of boating on Bison Lake and running three miles a day, he had to admit that he looked great. "Not bad for being forty-six years old," he said to no one in particular. In his mind he was just the right age to begin to make a name for himself. He got dressed in tan slacks with a pink dress shirt open at the collar and cordovan wing-tip shoes and headed out to begin his day. Next stop, the Ryerson Group Home.

Andrews lived in the posh suburb of Maple Grove at the end of a long and winding cul-de-sac. The two-story modern home was mostly steel and glass with a deck off the back family room that overlooked a wetland. The fact that he had no family wasn't lost on him. He'd never had time for one. Short-term affairs, yes; long term commitments, no. But he liked his big home and the prestige that went with it. He liked it a lot. Now, it was time to add to his possessions by getting an alien.

After breakfast of a cup of Earl Grey tea and a bowl of organic fruit, Andrews drove his white, one- year old Tesla twenty-miles to the group home, parked carefully at a diagonal to protect his precious car from getting dinged by some rude and inattentive driver, and got out. He grimaced at the neighborhood. Some would call it homey, he just called it tacky. Old 1930s and 1940s one and a half story well-kept bungalows along with a smattering of two- and three-story Victorians lined the street. Who needed all that old crap? Not Andrews. He liked things clean and neat. And modern.

He also liked the best that money could buy. He'd get that Kyle Johnson straightened out, that was for sure, and get rich in the process. He had it all set out in front of him, a plan that couldn't fail. He'd play along with the alien, get him to talk about life on whatever planet he came from, and record everything that was said. In maybe six months or so, while the case was still fresh in people's minds, he'd write a book. Then he and the alien would go on tour and hit the television and talk shows. Speaking fees would be enormous. He'd have to hire a business manager, maybe even an agent. Andrews smiled to himself. A year from now, he'd be famous. And rich.

Whistling softly as he went through the front door, the receptionist looked up and smiled. "Hi doctor Andrews. What brings he here this fine morning?"

Slightly perplexed, Andrews responded, "I'm here for Kyle Johnson. Slater should have told you I'd be here."

The receptionist, whose name tag said 'Amy', checked the appointment schedule on her computer and said, "I'm sorry, Doctor Andrews, but no one has told me anything. Would you like to talk to Ms. Simpson?" Amy pointed. "Her office is…"

Andrews felt his blood begin to boil and angerly cut her off. "Never mind. I know where her office is."

He stomped down the hall. Clara Simpson was a short, middle-aged woman, with close cropped grey hair, who'd been in the healthcare field for nearly thirty years. She'd seen it all and managed the Ryerson group home with a firm hand along with a kind and caring attitude.

She'd known Andrews for ten years and was on the phone with a vendor when he stormed into her office. She took one look at the red-faced doctor and spoke into the receiver, "Sorry. Something's come up. I'll call you back later." To Andrews she cracked a smile said, "Well, this is a surprise, Doctor. What can I do for you?"

Andrews could barely contain his fury. He leaned over her desk and said through clenched teeth, "What you can do," he pointed a finger at her, "is you can bring me to Kyle Johnson. I'm taking over his case. Slater should have told you."

Clara shook her head. "I'm sorry, but there must be some mis-understanding."

Andrews felt his blood begin to boil. "What misunderstanding?" he spat out. "That's impossible." He looked at his Rolex. "I'm supposed to pick him up here now, at nine." He turned to leave. "Forget it. I'll go get him myself."

He started to storm out of the office but stopped when Clara stood up and said, "I'm sorry, but you won't be able to do that."

Andrews turned to her and sneered. "Oh, really? Just watch me."

Clara stepped toward him from behind her desk, unwilling to be intimated by the man who towered over her by at least a foot and out-weighed her by nearly one-hundred pounds. She patiently explained, "It will be impossible because Kyle Johnson is not here."

"What!" Andrews exploded. "Not here! Where the hell is he?" His face began turning red and sweat started beading up on his forehead.

Clara stood calmly not three feet from the belligerent man. "You don't have to shout, Doctor Andrews."

"I'll shout if I want to!"

"Not in my presence you won't," she stated, looking at him straight in the eye, a look she'd used her entire career to calm unruly patients.

Her steely gaze cut into Andrews like a knife. He blinked once, then again, wiped his forehead, and said, "Well, okay. Sorry." His anger was barely contained. "But I need to speak to Kyle Johnson now. I'm going to be taking over his case."

"I'm sorry, but I don't know anything about that," Clara said. "All I can tell you is that Mr. Slater checked our Mr. Johnson late yesterday afternoon."

"What? That's impossible!" Clara shot him a look that made Andrews lower his voce. He gritted his teeth. "Do you know where were they going?"

"Mr. Slater said something about the Mayo Clinic. He was taking Mr. Johnson down there to have some tests run. They were going to keep him at the clinic overnight. Mr. Slater stayed down there with him." She stopped talking. "Doctor Andrews are you all right?"

Andrews had sat down in the only chair in the office. The Mayo Clinic was ninety-miles south of Ryerson in Rochester. What was Slater up to taking Johnson down there? Andrews pulled out his cell phone to make a call, and then realized where he was. He got to his feet and hurried out of Clara Simpson's office.

"I'm going to get to the bottom of this," he said over his shoulder.

Clara listened as Andrews charged down the hall, thinking, *there goes on screwed one up doctor. He could use some therapy himself.* Then she returned to her desk and picked up her phone to call the vendor back that she'd been talking with before Andrews had made his appearance. She quickly put the rude man out of her mind. She had work to do.

Outside in the parking lot, Andrews got into his car and called Jorgenson. "Phil," he said, when the call went through, "we've got a problem. Slater and Johnson have taken off."

Jorgenson listened to Andrews's rant for a few minutes, and then calmed him down by telling him that he'd take care of it. When Andrews was placated and had hung up, Jorgenson made a call to the Onus Brothers, Cletus, and Henry. He explained the situation to them, and they agreed to find what had happened. For a price.

Phil Jorgenson hung up and smiled. The Onus boys never let him down. He called Andrews back. "It's all taken care of," he said, and before Andrews could say anything, he disconnected. The more he thought about it, the more he was coming to the conclusion that his longtime friend, the doctor, was becoming slightly unhinged. If Andrews kept up acting like was, Jorgenson would have to do something about it.

Chapter Seventeen

JEREMY, EBAR, JULIE and Wren spent Thursday morning cooking a breakfast of scrambled eggs in the small kitchen in the RV and getting acclimated to their secluded campsite nestled in the pine trees along the shore of Lake Superior. Little did they know that by then Andrews had discovered Ebar and Jeremy were gone, and he'd called his friend Phil Jorgenson who had called the Onus brothers and put them on their trail.

The Onus brothers, Clete, and Henry made a living doing tasks other people wanted done but didn't want to do themselves. They specialized in tracking down bail jumpers for a couple of the bail bondsmen in south Chicago, and they'd been in the business for twenty-five years. And they were good at it. But they also had a darker, more violent side and saw no problem beating people up to teach them a lesson, something Phil Jorgenson has used them for on more than a few occasions.

Clete was the older of the two. At six feet five inches he was a big man with short, cropped hair and a trim mustache. His muscular physique was bolstered by a two-hour weightlifting workout at Jimmy's Gym in Cisero, a place he frequented daily.

Henry was just as tall but was slender and kept in shape by running three miles every day. He had long, dark brown hair he wore in a top-knot and was always clean shaven.

The brothers shared a small house on a tiny lot in Naperville just west of downtown Chicago. Clete was at the kitchen table cleaning his gun and having a cup of coffee when he took the call from Jorgenson a little after nine on Thursday morning. After he disconnected, he went into the living room where Henry was sitting on the couch and said, "We've got a job."

"What is it?" Henry asked, putting down the Chicago Tribune crossword puzzle he was working on.

"Somebody Phil knows needs us to find a couple of guys. In Minnesota of all places." He handed his brother a sheet of paper with the names *Jeremy Slater* and *Kyle Johnson* on it.

"Huh. Are they gay or something? You know I don't dig queers."

Clete laughed. "Doesn't sound like it. I guess Jorgenson's friend is pissed off at them about something." He flexed his muscles and cracked his fingers. "What do we care? He's paying us five-grand plus expenses."

Henry grinned. "Sounds good to me." He looked outside through a small window in their living room. "They say that Minnesota's the land of sky-blue waters. We could use a little vacation." He chuckled and studied the piece of paper in his hand. "I'll get right on it. Why don't you look into making plane reservations?" Henry stood up to go downstairs to their computer workstation set up along one wall in their basement. "Probably get a car, too."

"I'm on it."

Once downstairs, Henry booted up their computer system. He put the name Jeremy Slater into the tracking software he'd developed over the years. By the time Clete came down to check on him, he had what he needed.

"Find them?" Clete asked.

"Well, I found Jeremy Slater, if that's what you mean." He grinned at his older brother, giving him a hard time. "I'm assuming this Kyle character is with him.'

"Funny," Clete responded. He made a move to slug his brother in the arm but held off as Henry automatically formed two fists to retaliate. Instead, he pulled up a chair and sat down. "What'd you find?"

Henry pointed to the monitor. "That's where his cell phone is."

Clete looked. "Damn it, man, it's up near Canada. Out in the middle of nowhere."

Henry laughed. "Sort of. Look up Lake Superior on your phone. Look up Duluth, too. It's not so bad up there. Vacation land. Lots of tourists."

"Even now? After Labor Day?"

Henry thought about it and then said, "Well, no, probably not."

"That might work in our favor."

"Right. Less people around. Less eyes to see."

"The client just wants us to bring them back. Apparently, no rough stuff."

Henry laughed. "Well, a little rough stuff never hurt, you know. Just to make a point."

Clete grinned and cracked his knuckles. "Good. I could use a little workout."

"Well, it looks like you're going to get your chance. Did you make plane reservations?"

"Yeah. For Minneapolis. Flight leaves at noon. Should I change them for Duluth?"

Henry thought about it before saying, "No. That's not necessary. We've got plenty of time. Plus, I wouldn't mind seeing Minnesota again. It's been a while."

"That Baxter case, right?"

"Yeah. The guy should never have tried to run."

Clete grinned. "He'll never run again, not with that shattered kneecap."

"I don't think he expected you to shoot him there."

"All part of the job, little brother. All part of the job."

160

They both laughed.

Less than three hours later they were on a plane to the Minneapolis St. Paul International Airport. By one o'clock in the afternoon, they'd rented a white Fort Explorer and were on their way north.

Clete drove. He was wearing dark slacks, a white dress shirt and a dark blue sports coat to cover the .22 revolver with short loads in his shoulder holster. Henry monitored Jeremy on his laptop. He was dressed casually in red silk basketball shorts and a long-sleeve black tee-shirt. Clete wore brown penny loafers and no socks, and Henry wore white, high-end Adidas running shoes. Both men wore wraparound sunglasses.

Just south of Hinkley, Clete asked for the tenth time since they'd started driving, "That Slater dude still there?"

Henry sighed, "Yep. Still there."

"What do you think?"

"I think the guy is sitting tight. Probably in some campground. Maybe a cabin."

"How do you think he got there?"

"Drove you dummy. Geez."

"Well, he'll have a big surprise in store when we get there," Clete said, patting his gun under his arm. They'd easily gotten through TSA security by declaring it. No problem.

Henry turned to his brother. "I don't think the gun will be necessary. This Jeremy guy sounds like a wimp."

"Good," Clete grinned. But he patted his gun again, anyway, and said, "No matter what, though, I'm ready for whatever happens. At least it'll be fun to scare the crap out of the little shit."

Henry shook his head, "Big brother, you always seem to have a way with words."

Clete grinned. "Maybe I missed my calling."

"What's that?" Henry asked looking out the window at a dilapidated farmhouse with some cars and trucks rusting in the front yard, thinking, *who could ever live like that?*

"I could have been an English teacher," Clete said, glancing over at his younger brother. "Or a writer."

Henry looked at him and laughed. "A writer? Give me a break. You don't even like to read."

Clete was quiet for a moment, staring at the road ahead before saying, "What difference does that make?"

Henry laughed, "Yeah, you're probably right."

Clete put his turn signal on to pass a slow-moving pickup truck, giving the driver, an old man in beat up straw hat, the finger as he passed.

"Jerk," he muttered.

"Calm down. You can have some fun with this Jeremy guy when we find him. And that Kyle dude, too. I guess he's some psycho who thinks he's an alien."

Clete laughed. "Two for the price of one. All the better. When do you think we'll get there?"

"We'll stop in Duluth for a nice meal and then head up the north shore. We should be there by night fall. We'll take care of business and be back in Chicago tomorrow easy."

"Sweet. They'll never know what hit 'em."

Chapter Eighteen

AFTER BREAKFAST, THE four of them gathered at the picnic table, Jeremy and Ebar on one side across from Julie and Wren on the other. They sipped coffee (except for Ebar and his bottle of water) and talked about what they should do next; should they stay at the campsite and hope Andrews wouldn't be able to find them, or should they get back on the road and try to locate a better place to hide out? After half an hour of lively debate, they had no consensus of what they should do, or where they should go, and there was lull in the conversation.

Ebar took that moment to stand up. He said to them, "Say, do any of you guys' care if I go for a walk? I've got some stuff to think about."

Given Ebar's conversation the day before with commander Zenon in the mechanical room of the group home, it didn't surprise Jeremy in the least that his friend had things on his mind. "Sure," he said. "Where are you going?"

Ebar pointed through the trees to where the cove was just barely visible. "I'm going to go down to the lake and walk along the shore. I saw a big rock earlier over by the point up to the right. I might hike over there and sit on it for a while. Think a little."

"Sounds good. Got your phone?"

"Yes. Send me a text if you need me."

"Okay." Ebar waved good-bye to Jeremy and gave Julie and Wren each a hug. "I'll be back in a little while."

Jeremy had the feeling Ebar was going to try and contact Zenon. If that was the case...he looked at Julie and Wren. They were watching their alien friend walk to the woods and the trail leading down to the shore. He said, "Wren, I know Julie knows, but I've got something to tell you."

They both turned to him.

"What's up?" Wren asked, taking a sip of her coffee. Seeing the grim expression on Jeremy's face, she turned to Julie and joked, "I bet I know. I'll bet now is the time our pal Jeremy is finally going to spill the beans and tell us the truth; that he's really an alien, too, just like Ebar." Of the three of them, Wren was taking the idea of their adventure to heart and had been in a good mood ever since yesterday when she and Julie had decided to help out. She sipped again from her mug and grinned at him. "Okay, pal. Now's the time to come clean."

Jeremy was silent as he drank from his own mug. Across from him Wren was waiting with a smile on her face. Finally, he looked at her and said, "I appreciate the humor, I really do. But no, it's not that. I'm not an alien. But what I have to tell you serious. In fact, I should have told you earlier. But" he shook his head, "there was a lot to deal with."

"What is it?" Wren asked, suddenly concerned.

"It has to do with Ebar and Zenon."

"The Commander?"

Next to her Julie suddenly went pale. "Oh, no!"

"What?" Wren turned to her.

Julie moved closer and touched her partner's arm. "I should have told you more about this yesterday."

Wren quickly glanced back and forth between Julie and Jeremy. "Hey, will one of you please tell me what's going on?"

Julie pointed to Jeremy and said, "Better start with what happened in the mechanical room."

Jeremy took a deep breath and let it out. "Okay." He looked at Wren and said, "You know that Ebar's been sending those communiques of his for the entire time he's been on earth, right?"

"Right. That's what Julie said."

"Okay. And that this past summer, just before he got into

165

the fight at the treatment plant, his communiques quit being answered. Right?"

"Yeah, I'm aware of that. So what?"

"Well, yesterday, Zenon got in touch with Ebar."

"I know." Wren said and shrugged her shoulders. "Julie told me. A little bit anyway."

Next to her, Julie sucked in a deep breath and let it out. She turned to Jeremy and said, "I didn't go into a lot of detail. I was more concerned about Andrews at the time. You better tell her about everything about Zenon."

Jeremy cleared his throat. "Okay. There's a lot to it, so I'll give you the highlights. In a nutshell, the situation is pretty desperate. As far as I can make out, Zenon wants Ebar's opinion of whether or not now is a good time to take over earth. What Zenon wants to do is basically annihilate all human life and repopulate it with inhabitants from their home planet, Rykos."

Julie turned to Wren. "I'm so sorry." She got to her feet and wrung her hands in frustration. "I should have told you more yesterday. This is a big deal. In all the excitement getting Ebar away from Andrews, I guess I put the Zenon issue on the back burner." She took both of Wren's hands in hers. "I'm really sorry."

Wren got up and gave Julie a hug. "Hey, don't worry about it. What's past is past. Let's just focus on the here and now." She started pacing back and forth, thinking on her feet. "You're right, this thing with Zenon is huge. If Ebar is going to give the go ahead to attack earth..." Her words trailed off. She ran her fingers through her hair. "This is insane! I mean, I can go along with Ebar being an alien and

166

helping him to get his act together and all of that psychology stuff, but this is super crazy. An alien invasion of earth?" She looked at Jeremy. "Do you have any idea what he's going to do?"

"I don't. He's been pretty closed mouthed about it. All I know is that he's in a quandary. He wants to go home. But he likes me, and he's obviously getting to like you two." Jeremy pointed to Julie and Wren. "I'm pretty sure he'll do the right thing."

Wren got right in Jeremy's face. "But you don't know, right? You don't know what he's going to do, do you?"

Jeremy turned red from embarrassment. "Honestly, I don't. But I'll tell you this. I think we should try and find him. Right now. We all need to talk."

Julie spoke up, "That's right. We've got to find him and convince him to do everything in his power to stop this so-called invasion. I mean Ebar's a nice guy and all, but this Zenon sounds like a megalomaniac freak."

"Wren chimed in. "I agree. Totally."

Jeremy had guessed that this would be how they'd react, and he'd been right. He probably should have said something earlier, but at least the cards were on the table now. He got up from the picnic table. "Ebar was going to the point at the end of the cove. Let's see if we can find him and talk to him."

Julie started walking. "Okay. Let's go," she said.

"Hold on." Wren ran to the RV and ducked inside. She returned moments later with a pair of binoculars over her shoulder. "Okay," she said. "I'm all set."

167

They left their camping area and hurried together through the forest. A minute later they were standing at the trail leading down the twenty-foot embankment to the shore. From their high vantage point, they could see the entire cove with the shoreline extending in a crescent moon shape about a quarter of a mile in each direction. They saw no sign of Ebar. They descended to the shore and looked to the right hoping to see him, but the beach was deserted.

Wren raised her binoculars to look more closely. Then, disappointed, she lowered them. "I don't see a thing," she said. "Do you think he ran away? I'm wondering if maybe he took off and we'll never see him again. That would not be good."

"Let's get to the point," Jeremy said, "and see what we can find out."

The pebbles making up the shoreline were not the easiest to walk on, but they hurried as fast as they could to the point. When they got there, they found no trace of Ebar, nor signs that he'd been there. The place was vacant. Beyond the point the coast extended nearly a hundred miles to the south, all the way to Duluth, a foreboding shoreline littered with rocks and boulders and scrub pine and windblown downed trees that made it nearly impossible to walk.

"Jeremy climbed a large nearby rock, shielded his eyes from the sun and looked to the south. He didn't see Ebar. Wren used her binoculars and scanned up and down the shoreline and, like Jeremy, saw nothing. Julie joined them and looked and looked but, she, too, saw no sign of Ebar.

They all called his name, "Ebar! Ebar! Come on back!!" Not a word in return.

Jeremy sent a text. No response. He sent another one. Nothing.

Finally, Jeremy said, "Damn! It looks like he took off. I can't believe it." He kicked at a small pebble sending it rolling into the water. "And here I trusted him."

Julie said, "Look, don't beat yourself up. Like you said, in order to communicate with Zenon, he needs a quiet place where he can concentrate."

Jeremy's mood suddenly brightened. "Hey, that's right." He looked around at the forest surrounding them. It was made up of as many free-standing trees as ones that had fallen due to high water and storms. He waved his arm in a circle encompassing the lake in front of them and the forest behind them. "I'm sure there are lots of secluded places around there like that." Then he paused, thinking, before adding, "But I'm concerned about what he's going to tell Zenon. What if he tells that fruitcake to attack? Then we're done for." He snapped his fingers. "Gone. Just like that."

Wren asked, "Do you really think he' do that and suggest they attack? Ebar seemed so happy being here and hanging out with us."

Jeremy answered, "Oh, he was happy, alright. Or is happy. Whatever the case, I could just tell." He pointed to the big lake. "He obviously loved being here at the campground and close to Lake Superior." He looked at Julie and Wren. "What about you two? You could tell he was happy, right?" The two of them silently nodded in agreement.

Then Julie spoke up. "What's you biggest concern?"

Jeremy didn't have to think. "That Zenon sounds like a

powerful personality. Ebar is pretty naïve and trusting. Who knows what Zenon could talk him into?"

Wren looked out over the big lake, and then turned to her friends and said, "Well, we did the right thing for him by getting him out from underneath the clutches of Andrews. Hopefully, Ebar with do the right thing by us."

"What's that?" Julie asked.

Wren gave her a wry smile. "To tell this Zenon guy to basically shove it."

In spite of their dire situation Julie and Jeremy both laughed. Then they headed back to the campground to wait for Ebar to return. They hoped so, anyway. If he didn't come back, they all knew one thing - it meant that Ebar had turned his back on his friends, and that their time on earth was essentially over.

Chapter Nineteen

WHEN JEREMY, JULIE and Wren were standing on the point looking and calling for Ebar, he was watching them the entire time. Earlier, he figured they'd eventually come looking for him, and he didn't want to be found, so he'd done the unexpected. He'd found a tall pine tree and climbed it. The branches were close enough together to make the going relatively easy, plus they hid him well. He climbed about thirty feet until he found a branch thick enough to sit on. He propped his back up against the truck of the tree and looked out over the vast expanse of Lake

Superior. He was near to the point, close enough that he could see his friends when they showed up. He felt badly that they were frightened by what he had to do, but he'd deal with them later. Now that they'd left, he prepared himself to contact Zenon.

He closed his eyes and centered himself by focusing on his breathing, in and out, in and out. He opened up his senses, hearing birds calling and the buzzing of insects and the gentle breeze off the lake softly whispering through the pine needles. He breathed in the scent of lake water and pine needles and the musky aroma of decaying vegetation. He let his mind drift and refocus until he saw himself back on Rykos at the reservoir.

Then he went deep within himself to the depths of his soul, and he was aware of nothing. He was waiting.

Suddenly, a vision of commander Zenon appeared. He spoke in a deep voice, "So, Ebar, what news do you have for me? Shall I give the orders to attack, and have it done with? Shall we begin our takeover earth?"

Ebar had volunteered for the mission to come to earth because he'd had nothing much going on in his life. And that had been true. He'd been young, in his early twenties in earth years, and was looking for an adventure. He'd been on earth for fifty years now. He had hitch-hiked from California to Minnesota and settled in the small town of Orchard Lake. He'd found a job at the hardware story and then the sewage treatment plant. He'd sent communiques about life in the United States and Orchard Lake in particular on a regular basis. Even though he hadn't made a lot of friends, he was well liked and was considered a valued member of the community. In Ebar's mind, he had

172

done an admirable job of balancing his alien duties of observation and regular communication back to Rykos, with his earthly duties of working and being a good citizen in Orchard Lake.

Then during this past summer he'd lost communication with Zenon. He'd gotten worried about being stranded on earth and never going home again. Then he'd gotten into the fight with Al, a fight many people, Jeremy and his boss Lou included, thought was justified. But Al had brought charges, the police had locked him in jail, and he'd made the mistake of trying to talk to Zenon. The jailer had overheard him, reported him to the proper authorities, and he'd been transferred to the Buffalo County Hospital and the psych ward when he'd been medicated and put under observation. Who knows what would have happened if Jeremy hadn't shown up?

Jeremy. Ebar smiled, thinking of the young, bearded, idealistic mental health worker. Only on the job for a few weeks, Ebar was his first case. They had gotten along well, and Ebar began to trust that Jeremy would truly help him. And he did. Not only did the young counselor come to believe Ebar was the alien he said he was, but Jeremy also had the courage to go bat for him in that last meeting.

Ebar thought back. That fateful meeting had been only yesterday, but it seemed so much longer ago than that. Their lives had changed forever. Andrews had wanted to take over Ebar's case, and Jeremy wouldn't let him. With Julie's help, along with her partner, Wren, they'd made their escape. Now, here they were. On the north shore of Lake Superior in the Northwoods of Minnesota. Ebar had fallen in love with the lake the first time he'd seen it, or sensed it's presence, rather, last night coming into Duluth over the bluffs high above the huge expanse of water. He felt it then, and he felt it now, an incredible connection, a natural bonding of sorts, that seemed be drawing him to the mighty lake. He felt at home here, like he truly belonged. He never wanted to leave.

But then there was commander Zenon. He didn't care one small bit about Ebar and his feelings regarding his life on earth and how fondly he felt toward his friends. Not at all. Instead, all he wanted was Ebar's cold and calculated take on the situation. If Ebar gave the go-ahead, then the commander would give the attack order and all humanity on earth, including Jeremy, Julie, and Wren, would be wiped out. Could Ebar live with that? He didn't have to think long. Or hard. The answer was no.

On the other hand, Zenon was a powerful force. If Ebar said 'Yes, commander, go ahead and give the order,' Zenon would. And that would be it. No more life on earth. Ebar would be whisked back immediately to Rykos and his life there would go on. Would it be different? Probably. He'd most certainly be considered a hero. Did he want that? The answer was simple. No, he did not. He'd never been one for the limelight and didn't like attention being drawn to him. So, if that was the case, what did he want? Well, the longer he was on the North Shore with Jeremy and his new friends, Julie and Wren, the answer was becoming clear. He wanted to live here by the big lake. In fact, he wanted to live the rest of his life here.

Ebar's thoughts were interrupted by commander Zenon. "Ebar. Come in. Ebar. Where are you? Are you still there?"

"Yes, sir. I'm here."

"Do you have a decision? I'm in the mood to attack. If not earth, I've got a few other planets in mind."

Ebar took a deep breath to center himself. Then he spoke with as much confidence as he could muster, "Sir, I'm sorry to say, but I don't think earth is a good fit for us."

"Really. I'm surprised. They have so much water. Why is it that you say that?"

"Well, when I arrived in 1967 the water supply was pretty good."

"That's what I remember you saying."

"Yes. It was. But I have to say that over the years the planet earth has changed significantly. There's global warming and the average temperature is increasing and that's having drastic environmental effects."

"I can imagine. But what about the water?"

"The water has become horribly polluted, sir. The population on earth had increased by nearly two billion people since I've been here, and they have all contributed to water pollution. It's pretty bad. And it makes me sad to say this, but I don't think earth is suitable for our needs. It would be too costly to clean up this planet to make it livable for us."

"So, what are you saying? Get to the point."

"What I'm saying is that I recommend we pass on taking over earth. I'm sure they are better planets out there."

Commander Zenon was quiet for a moment. Ebar broke out in a cold sweat. Had he over-stepped his bounds? Had he made Zenon mad? He held his breath waiting.

Finally, Zenon spoke. "Well, I must say that I'm

175

disappointed."

"I'm sorry, sir…"

"Let me finish. I'm disappointed, but I understand what you are saying. I don't want to waste resources there if I don't need to."

"I'm happy to hear that, sir," Ebar said. He exhaled and began breathing relatively normally again. To say he was relived was putting it mildly.

Zenon continued. "I've got another planet all picked out. We'll go with that one."

"That sounds good, sir." Even though it didn't sound so good for the inhabitants of that planet. But Ebar was not one to argue with his commander.

Then Zenon dropped a bombshell. "So, I guess that means your mission is over, Ebar. You've been there for fifty years, and that's a long time. I'm sure you miss being on Rykos. You can come home anytime you like."

"Sir?"

"Yes, you can come home. Didn't you hear me?"

What Ebar heard was Zenon being done with their conversation and wanting to move on to other things. He was not a patient man.

"Come home?"

"Yes. There is a time-space portal located in a place called the Black Hills. You can use that. I'll keep it open for you for twenty days." Ebar did a quick calculation. Twenty days would be around the first week of October. "You'll have until then to come home. If not," here he lowered his voice and continued ominously, "the portal will close, and you will be left on earth for the rest of your life. Is that understood?"

"Yes, sir. It's understood."

And with that Zenon broke the connection.

Ebar sat in the tree and looked out over Lake Superior. The wind was picking up and his tree was gently swaying. He liked the motion of the tree trunk moving back and forth, back, and forth. It was a happy feeling.

From his high vantage point, he could see waves forming far out on the lake. Long lines of white-caps were marching across the horizon heading toward land to eventually come crashing onto the shore. The longer he watched the water, the more Ebar gained strength from it, strength he knew he'd need in the upcoming days. Should he stay on earth or return to Rykos? He had a good idea what he'd do, but first he had to get back to camp and tell the others of his conversation with Zenon. He had a feeling they'd be interested.

He started the long climb to the ground, thinking how much he loved being in the woods and near Lake Superior. No matter what happened in the days ahead, he knew one thing for certain, he'd find a way to come back. That was for sure.

**

While Ebar had been talking to commander Zenon, two hours away in Duluth, Clete was pulling the rented white Ford SUV into the parking lot of The Black Bear, a restaurant known for its cedar-plank seared steaks. Henry had found it on the internet.

"Says here it's the best steak in northern Minnesota," he said, reading off the website. "What do you think?"

Clete grinned. "Sounds good to me. We'll get a good meal in us, and then go take care of that Slater dude and that nutcase with him."

Henry laughed. "Yeah, should be an easy job. Those two sound like they'll be a pushover."

The restaurant was halfway up the bluff overlooking the city, and there was a panoramic view of Lake Superior from the parking lot. The Onus brothers didn't notice. All they cared about right then was food. Clete turned off the car and went to get out. The wind came up and it taught the heavy door and banged it hard against the side of the vehicle.

"Damn!" Clete said, catching hold of the door and slamming it shut. "Let's inside out of this wind. I'm starving."

Henry stowed his laptop under the seat and noticed that Clete was still wearing his gun. *Oh, well,* he thought to himself. *Whatever makes him happy.* "Hold on," he said. "I'm right behind you."

Clete clasped Henry on the shoulder as they headed for the front door and said, "I'm looking forward to this."

Henry looked at him and they crunched across the gravel parking lot and asked, "What? The meal? Or the job?"

Clete grinned and rubbed the handle of his gun, barely

hidden under his sports jacket. "Both, little brother. Both."

Chapter Twenty

BACK AT THE campground, to say Jeremy and Julie and Wren were concerned over the recent turn of events with Ebar was putting it mildly.

"I can't believe he just left us," Jeremy said, picking up a pinecone and throwing it a tree. Then he picked up another one and threw it, too. They both missed. "Damn," he swore.

He was picking up a third one when Julie grabbed his arm and stopped him. "Just calm down, my friend, before you destroy the entire forest."

"I'm just pissed off," Jeremy spat out. "I never expected him to do this." He sat down at the picnic table and twisted the top off a bottle of water like he was twisting the neck off a chicken.

Julie looked at Jeremy with raised eyebrows, then turned to Wren and said, "I don't think any of us did."

Wren, who had been standing by the RV studying her phone, looked up and nodded. "No kidding." She walked over and joined Jeremy at the picnic table. Julie sat down, too. Soon, the three of them were in a heavy conversation.

So much so that they didn't see Ebar when he showed up.

"Hi everyone," he said, smiling his most pleasant smile. He knew they'd be angry at him and wanted to try and set a pleasing tone. It almost worked.

Jeremy was not swayed. He jumped to his feet with his fists clenched. "What were you thinking, going off like that? We were worried about you."

Ebar put up his hand in a placating manner. "I know. I so sorry. I just needed to get away for a while. Have some 'me time' as people say."

Wren could see right through Ebar's smokescreen. "That's a bunch of BS," she said. "We know what you were up to."

Ebar glanced at Jeremy with a questioning look. Jeremy responded by saying, "I told her, Ebar. I told her about you and Zenon."

Ebar gasped. "Everything?"

"Yes, everything," Julie piped up. She got to her feet and

stood right in front of him, pointing a finger. "Let's get one thing straight right now, mister. If we're going to help you, you've got to be honest with us. Okay? All of us."

"That's right," Wren added, leaving the picnic table, and joining her. "We've all put our lives on the line for you."

Ebar wrung his hands. "And I appreciate that, I really do. I'm very sorry."

Jeremy's anger had dissipated. He could see how worried Ebar was that he'd made his friends so concerned, not to mention angry. He got up, stepped close and put his hand on his friend's shoulder. "So, what did you tell him anyway? This Zenon guy? What'd you say to him?"

Ebar pointed to the picnic table. "How about if we all sit down? This might take a while." They did, and he told them the whole story. And he told them the truth.

It was early evening when he finished. When he was done, Jeremy grinned. "You told him the earth's water supply was polluted? That was brilliant." He was relieved. For a while there he thought he'd made a huge mistake in believing Ebar. Now he was glad that he had trusted him. In the end, Ebar had done what they all hoped he would do. He'd done the right thing.

"Yeah. I told him about global warming, too. I tried to get the point across that the planet earth was a mess and not worth the price and resources it would take to fix it."

Wren said, "So you told him the truth." Everyone laughed at her dark humor.

Ebar grinned. "Yes. I did."

"And he was good with that?" Jeremy asked.

183

"Yes, he was," Ebar said.

"So, no worries about commander Zenon and commandos from Rykos ever attacking and taking over earth? We're done with that discussion?"

"Yes, we are," replied Ebar. Then he was quiet.

Jeremy immediately picked up on his friend's mood. "What's up? There's something else isn't there?"

"Well, yes, there is. It has to do with me going back to Rykos. I only have…"

Ebar was interrupted by a car entering their space in the campground. It was a large, white SUV and it parked right behind the RV.

"What's going on?" Wren asked, standing up from the picnic table.

Julie joined her and said, "I don't know."

Jeremy got up and so did Ebar. The two of them started walking toward the SUV. Jeremy said, "I'll go find out what the deal is."

Wren and Julie joined him. Wren said, "Us to."

Jeremy appreciated their support. "Good," he said.

Ebar was walking next to Jeremy. "You think this has to do with you taking me? What you call kidnapping?"

Jeremy didn't have to think. "Yeah, I do," he said. He looked at Julie and Wren. "What do you guys think?"

Julie spoke first. "I think you're right."

"Me, too," said Wren.

Ebar adjusted his glasses and looked at Jeremy. "Okay.

Like I saw in a movie once, I guess it's show time. Let's go see what this is all about."

Chapter Twenty-One

AFTER A MEAL meal of two-inch thick bloody steaks and two ice cold beers each, Clete had made good time driving north from Duluth. They found the campground around seven o'clock that evening.

"That's it," Henry said, pointing to the sign and consulting the signal on his laptop. "The guy is in there somewhere."

Clete pulled off the highway and coasted to a stop just outside the entrance. He looked at the sign and smirked,

"*Cozy Cove*. What a stupid name for a campground."

Henry glanced up from his computer. "Hey, it's Minnesota. Northern Minnesota at that. They do a lot of stupid things in this state. Look at their football team."

Clete grunted and laughed. "Yeah, they suck big time. That's for sure." He peered through the windshield into the thick pine forest. It was deep in shadow, so he took off his sunglasses to see better. So did Henry. "But help me out here, little brother. Which way do I go?"

Henry looked at his screen and then pointed. "Go straight. There's a map here. I'll guide you."

Clete pulled slightly ahead and pointed. "There's a paybox."

Henry laughed. "So what?"

"Right." Clete grinned and kept going. He drove slowly, looking from side to side. "Not many campers. That's good."

"Lots of trees," Henry remarked.

"Yep. Nice and private." Clete turned to his brother. "We like private, don't we?"

"Exactly," Henry said. After a minute or two of winding through the pine forest, he pointed. "See that RV up there? I think that's it."

"I thought the little pansy drove a Honda?"

"Well, that's what my information said. An old beater of a Honda Civic." He checked the screen of his laptop. "Whatever the case. He's here."

"His phone is here."

"Right." Henry pointed to a group of people near a picnic table. "But take a gander. I'm pretty it's that Slater dude."

Clete looked as he pulled in behind the RV and parked. "The guy with the beard?"

"Yeah. That's him. I got his picture off his driver's license."

"Who's the other guy?"

"That skinny little geek with the glasses? He must be the nutcase we have to bring back."

"What are we going to do about the guy with the beard?"

"That's up to him."

Clete pointed. "What's with the two women?"

"I don't know. No one said anything about women."

Clete looked at Henry and grinned. "They look nice. Maybe we could use that RV. Have a little fun."

Henry shut the laptop and smiled back. "I like your thinking, big brother. I like it a lot."

Clete shut off the engine and opened the door. "All right then. Let's go earn our money. All set?"

Henry slid the laptop beneath the seat. "Yep. Got your gun?"

Clete patted under his arm. "You bet."

"Let's go."

***

189

Jeremy stopped walking when he saw the two big guys get out of the SUV. His first thought was *Thugs*. He turned to Ebar and said, "Watch out. This could be it."

Ebar was on his left, and in a moment Julie and Wren were standing on his right. Julie whispered to him. "What do you think?"

"I think Andrews hired these guys to find us, and they did."

"Think there'll be trouble?"

"Yes. I have a bad feeling about this," Jeremy said out of the side of his mouth."

He noticed Wren whispered something to Julie who nodded, but before he could ask her about it, the two guys started walking toward them.

The tall, thin one in red satin basketball shorts smiled and said, "Hi there. Nice evening, isn't it?"

"Yeah, it is," Jeremy said, stepping cautiously forward. "What can we do for you guys?"

With ten feet separating the two groups, the men stopped walking. The heavy-set guy with a shaved head said, "What can do, jerk, is you can come with us." Then, he pointed at Ebar and added, "And bring your little buddy, too. You both get in our car, the four of us drive off and they'll be no trouble."

Jeremy laughed nervously. "What?" He looked at Ebar and Julie and Wren standing a few feet behind him. "No. I don't think so."

The heavy-set guy pulled out a gun and pointed it at

Jeremy. "I think different."

"Jesus!" Jeremy spat out. "What's going on here?" Although he knew full well what was going on. Andrews had obviously sent people out to look for them. And they'd been found.

Clete took three quick steps forward, and, without warning, pistol whipped Jeremy across the side of the head. "Shut up, jerk face. Quit asking questions and do what I tell you."

Jeremy fell to his knees and put his hand to his head. It came away bloody. He felt sick to his stomach, but he held it down. Despite his size, he'd never been a violent person, but now he was getting mad.

Ebar knelt next to him and said, "Here let me help you up."

Clete and Henry watched the goings on with bemused smiles.

"Oh, isn't that sweet?" Clete remarked, as Ebar helped Jeremy to his feet and tried to stop the blood flowing from the wound. "Why don't you kiss it and make it all better?"

Julie glared at him and grabbed a napkin from the picnic table. She was about to hand it to Ebar when Henry said, "Hold it there, sister. Stay right where you are."

"But he's hurt," Julie said, taking a step forward.

Quick as a cat, Clete tossed the gun to Henry and grabbed her. "Didn't you hear my brother, you little bitch?"

She squirmed and tried to get away. "Let go of me, you creep!"

Clete slapped her hard, and she quit struggling. "Time to

teach you a lesson, girly." He pulled her toward the RV and said over his shoulder to Henry. "Watch over these other three. Little sister and I are going to get to know each other better." He pawed at her chest and grinned at his brother. "I might be awhile." Then he opened the door and pushed Julie inside, slamming the door shut behind them.

Henry watched his brother with interest. After the two of them disappeared into the RV, he turned and looked at his three captives. His eyes latched onto Wren. "I think when he's done with her, I'm going to take you inside. How'd you like…"

He never finished his sentence because he was interrupted by Clete's ear-piercing screams.

"Owwwww. God damnit, you bitch! What did you do to me? Oh, my god, I can't see."

Henry looked at the RV and yelled, "Clete! Clete!! What's going on?"

"Owww. Oh, man. Help me!"

Henry threatened his captives with the gun. "You three stay right where you are and don't move. I have no problem using this thing." He hurried to the RV, threw open the door and was stepping inside when Julie sprayed him square in the eyes with her can of pepper spray, a can they kept hidden but easily accessible near the door. "Owwww. My god. I'm blinded!!" He brought his hands to his face and covered his eyes. In the process, he dropped his gun.

Wren hurried to pick it up. "Got it." Then she pointed the gun at Henry and said, "On your knees, big boy. I've got you covered." She risked a glance at Jeremy and Ebar who were watching the proceedings in awe. She smiled, "Wow.

That's felt good. I've always wanted to stay that."

While Wren kept watch over Henry, Ebar grabbed some more napkins off the picnic table and used them to stop Jeremy's bleeding.

Then the two of them helped Julie muscle Clete out of the RV. They pushed him to the ground next to his brother, both men writhing in pain.

Ebar watched them for a moment, and then said, "We should tie them up or something."

Wren used the gun and made a motion toward the RV. "There's rope in the storage bin behind the front wheel. Why don't you get it, and I'll keep an eye on these two."

"I'm on it." Ebar hurried to get the rope and brought it back, saying to Jeremy and Julie, "Why don't you guys help me tie them up? Hands behind the back first and then their feet."

Five minutes later, with the two men securely bound, Jeremy pointed to the picnic table. "Let's sit down over there and figure out what to do."

Wren brought out some bottled water from the RV and the four of them sat looking at their two captives. "Any ideas?" she asked handing out the water.

Jeremy spoke up, "I'm pretty sure these guys were sent by Andrews. What do you all think?"

"Definitely Andrews sent them," Julie said. "But let's ask them." She raised her voice. "Hey, you two. Who sent you?"

Clete spoke up, apparently for both of them, and yelled, "Shut up, you bitch! You're getting nothing from us."

Julie grinned at the two men. "Pretty big talk for two

guys who got taken down by a bunch of amateurs." They both let loose a string of profanities at her. She turned to her friends, "Well, that answers that. So, what are we going to do?"

"We can't let them go, right?" Wren asked. "They'll just tell Andrews where we are"

"Yeah," Jeremy said, touching his wound. Julie had ripped up a dishtowel and wrapped it around his head. Only a tiny spot of blood was showing through. "Obviously, we can't have that." He was quiet for a minute, thinking. Finally, he said, "I'm drawing a blank. I just don't know what to do."

Ebar spoke up. He'd been quiet, listening to the back-and-forth talk. Finally, he said, "Well, don't forget, I'm an alien."

In spite of the tense situation, Jeremy grinned. "No, my friend, believe me, none of us have forgotten. Why?"

"Well, I do have special powers, you know. Stuff none of you have ever seen before."

All three sets of eyes turned to him. Wren was the first to speak, "Like what?" she asked.

"Well...I'll show you." He stood up and motioned to the others. "Follow me."

Clete and Henry had been propped up against the side of the RV. The effect of the pepper spray was wearing off, but their eyes were red and wet from the tears pouring out of them. Ebar motioning for the others to say behind as he approached to within about five feet.

Clete looked up. "What the hell do you want, you little

freak?"

Ignoring the comment, Ebar politely asked, "Do either of you gentlemen want any water? We've got some nice cool bottled water here for you. It'll taste good. I'm sure you're thirty."

Clete looked at Henry who shook his head 'no'. Then he stared at Ebar through his red bloodshot eyes and said, "Don't pull any of that psychology crap on us and try to get on our good side. You just don't get it do you? You're in big trouble. We were sent here to bring you back. If we don't do that, they'll send someone else. Maybe a bunch of people. Your done for."

Ebar contemplated that statement, and then said. "How about this? How about if we let you go, and you go back and tell them that you found us, but that there's nothing to worry about. That we're not a threat, and that they should just leave us alone. Could you do that for us? Please?"

In spite of being tied up and still smarting from the full force of the pepper spray, both Clete and Henry laughed. Henry said, "Man you guys are stupid. You're lives are over. Just let us go, we'll take you back and no one gets hurt." He looked at Wren and said, "I won't even bother with miss trigger-finger over there." He looked at Clete who nodded in agreement. "That's the deal. Take it or leave it."

Clete added. "I'd take it, if I were you."

Ebar turned to his three friends and said, "You heard the men. That's the deal. Do we take it?" All three of them shook their heads in the negative. No.

Ebar turned back to the Onus brothers. "Last chance.

Will you help us or not?"

"No," said Henry.

"Double no," said Clete.

"Okay," said Ebar. "Sorry hear that."

Ebar took a step back, folded his hands and closed his eyes. Afterwards, Jeremy, Julie, and Wren would say it was like he was gathering energy from some internal place deep inside. Whatever the case, they watched as their alien friend stood still for about a minute. Then he tilted his head back, spread his arms wide to the sky and uttered the phrase, "Abi-Aba-Nominin." And, just like that, Clete and Henry disappeared.

Chapter Twenty-Two

AFTER A MOMENT of stunned silence, Jeremy and Julie and Wren ran to the spot where they'd last seen the Onus Brothers. The ground was the same as it had been with not a twig or spec of dirt having been moved. It was like Clete and Henry had never been there.

"My god, Ebar, what did you do?" Jeremy asked. To be honest he didn't know if he was happy or mad or what.

Julie said, "Jeremy. Don't berate Ebar. He saved us. Those jerks were going to rape me and Wren and take both you two back to Andrews." She gave Ebar a tight hug. "He's a hero in my book."

And Ebar was. That was the way Jeremy finally began to look at the incident, which became *The Incident at Cozy Cove* in the days and weeks that followed. But there were still a few things to clear up.

Wren said, "What about their car? It's probably a rental. Should we drive it back? Drop it off somewhere?"

Julie said, "Both good ideas. How about this? Why don't we take the license plates off the rental and put them on our RV? That way if someone starts looking for us, they won't be able to track us by our license number. It might buy us a little time until we decide what to do."

"I'm all for it," Jeremy said. Then he pointed to the big white SUV? What about their vehicle?"

Julie looked at Ebar. "Magic time?"

He grinned. "Sure."

They took the plates off the rental and put them on the RV. Then they stood near the picnic table and watched as Ebar walked over close to the SUV and closed his eyes, concentrating. A minute later, he raised his hands to the sky and said, "Abi-Aba-Nominin". In a blink of an eye, just like with Clete and Henry, the vehicle disappeared, and with it, all traces of the Onus Brothers were forever gone.

By then night had fallen, and the stars were coming out. "Let's build a fire," Jeremy suggested, "and figure out what we're going to do next." The others agreed, and he soon had a nice blaze going in the fire ring. Julie and Wren brought out four camp chairs from the RV, and they made themselves comfortable with bottles of water.

After a few minutes staring into the flames, Jeremy asked, "So now what?"

Julie spoke up, "Well, obviously, you and Ebar need to stay on the run. You can't go back to Ryerson. You've got to stay one or two steps ahead of Andrews. The chances of him giving up on finding you and Ebar are slim to none and slim just left town."

"Yeah," Wren added. "Once he figures out something happened to those two thugs, he'll probably send more thugs. Ones that are smarter than those two." She pointed to the empty space on the ground by the RV. "Maybe even more vicious."

"I agree," Julie said. She looked at Jeremy. "Any ideas?"

"Not really." He signed and looked into the flames. "Canada?" He looked to the north. "It's not that far away." Dejectedly, he shook his head. "I just don't know." He took a drink of water, then picked up a nearby stick and poked at one of the burning logs. "How about you guys? So far no one knows you've helped us. You could leave us here and go camping out west like everyone thought you were going to do. No one would be any the wiser."

Wren spoke up. "That's right. Well, tomorrow's Friday. Technically, it's Julie's second day of vacation. As far as Andrews is concerned, we're on our way to Yellowstone Park for two weeks."

Jeremy looked at Julie. "Do you think he'll suspect you of helping me?"

"I don't know, maybe. He knows we're friends. You're gone. Ebar, um, Kyle, is gone. I'm gone. If he goes to the police, they might put two and two together."

"God, I'm so sorry," Jeremy said. "I didn't think it'd come to this."

Julie put her arm around his shoulder. "Don't worry about it. Me and Wren chose to do this." She turned to her lover. "Right?"

"Right." Wren looked at Jeremy. "And remember that Andrews is a pompous jerk who was going to make a mockery out of friend Ebar here." She pointed at Ebar with her thumb causing him to blush. "Also, always remember this - when all is said and done, it was the right thing to do."

Jeremy felt better hearing his friends talk, like a pep-talk his coach would have given before a big game back when he was in high school. "Thanks a lot, you guys. That helps. Although I still don't know what we're going to do."

Ebar spoke up. "Can I say something?" The three of them turned to him. "I've got something to tell you all. It's kind of a big deal for me."

"What's up?" Jeremy asked. With the annihilation of earth by troops from Rykos no longer a threat, he had put Ebar's problems on the back burner. That being said, at that very moment he suddenly realized he had forgotten there was still one big issue his friend the alien was faced with. Was Ebar going to go back to Rykos or not?

And that's exactly what Ebar wanted to talked about. He said, "There's no sense beating around the bush so here goes. Zenon said that I have twenty days to decide if I want to go home or not."

For a moment it was so quiet you could hear a pin drop. Then Jeremy, Julie and Wren started talking at once. After a minute, Ebar put up his hand. "Hold on, everyone. Let's take it one step at time. First off, Jeremy. What do you think I should do?"

In the less than two months he had known Ebar, Jeremy had come to not only like him a lot but to consider as a friend, the best friend he'd ever had. If Ebar left, he'd miss him terribly. But this was more than about his feelings, it was about Ebar's feelings, too. After thinking for a minute, he said, "Well, I hate to say it, because I'll miss you terribly, my friend, but if you have that option to go back, you should take it. It's the safest thing for you to do. That way you'll never have to worry about Andrews and getting caught by him and being put on display like some freak." It was breaking Jeremy's heart to say those words, but he felt they needed to be said. He continued, "Besides, you get to go home. You told me just last week that's what you wanted to do more than anything. Now you get to do it. That's a good thing, right?"

Instead of answering, Ebar turned to Julie and Wren. "What do you guys think?"

Wren spoke first. "I'd love for you to stay with us, but Jeremy's right. Going back is the safest thing to do."

"I agree," Julie said. "Plus, we've got the RV. We could easily drive you there." She pointed west toward where the Black Hills lay nearly one-thousand miles away. Then she quickly turned her head to the side so Ebar wouldn't see her wipe away the tears forming in her eyes. She'd miss him. She'd miss him a lot. She glanced at Wren who was barely holding back her own tears.

Jeremy spoke up. "Well, Ebar, as you can probably tell, we all really want you to stay, but the smartest thing to do is to go. Go home to Rykos. If you stay here, you and I will be on the run for the rest of our lives. It'll be hard. We'll constantly be looking over our shoulders and having to watch our backs. We'll never be able to settle down. It'll be…"

"Sorry to interrupt," Ebar said, "But I have to say something."

Jeremy looked over at his friend. "What is it?"

Ebar smiled, looked around the circle and said, "Thank you all so much for your input. It means the world to me, it really does. And it makes my decision even easier."

Jeremy held his breath.

"I've already decided, and what I've decided is that I don't want to go back."

Jeremy leaped to his feet and ran to Ebar so fast he knocked his chair over. "Yea!" he said and gave his friend a big hug.

Julie and Wren were right behind him.

Epilogue

And, true to his word, Ebar didn't go back to Rykos.

That night at the campfire the four of them agreed that staying on the road was a good thing to do, so the next day they took the RV to Yellowstone Park, like Julie and Wren had planned all along. They took their time getting there and even stopped at the Badlands in South Dakota on the way. The rocky landscape was interesting with its jagged hills and striated rock formations, but Ebar was nervous about the lack of water. Wren, who was driving, said, "Okay, my friend, we'll push on." And they did, getting to

Yellowstone later the next day. They found a secluded campsite on a small lake and spent a quiet ten days there, as peaceful and uneventful a time as they ever could have imagined.

Upon returning from vacation, Julie resigned from her job as a mental health professional in Bison County. She took time off from work, and she and Wren put their home in Minneapolis on the market, selling it within a month. Later that fall, the two of them moved to Duluth where Julie found a job with a hospice care provider, and Wren continued her graphic arts design business. They bought a lovely cottage style home on the north side of the city which was on steep hill and had a tremendous view of Lake Superior less than two miles away. They both agreed that life was better than it'd ever been.

Al dropped his charges against Kyle. It happened right after Lou took him to the Hitch' Post one night after work that September. "Yeah, we just had a nice little heart to heart talk," Lou told anyone who asked about it. "After I was done with him, Al thought it'd be a good idea." The fact that Lou unconsciously rubes his knuckles when talking about the *conversation* rarely goes unnoticed. Al still works at the facility, but he's lots of quieter these days, and more subdued, much to everyone's relief.

Of course, Doctor Richard Andrews was suspicious about the disappearance of both Ebar and Jeremy, but there was nothing he could do about it. With Jeremy and Kyle (Ebar) missing and unable to be found, he implored the police to, as he put it, "Check out that Julie character. She's up to no good, I just know it." But the cops didn't want to touch the case, especially when Andrews mentioned that there was a guy involved who thought he was an alien. There was no evidence of wrong-doing. The charges had been dropped by Al, so if Jeremy and Kyle wanted to go away and not be found there was no law saying they couldn't, no matter how incensed it made Andrews. Besides, after talking to Jeremy's mother, the police found out he was in regular communication with his parents and his brother. "He calls every few weeks or so," Mrs. Slater told the police. "I'm not worried at all." Like the lead detective told Andrews, "Look, they're adults. They can do whatever they want. You'll just have to learn to live with it." Which was not what Andrews wanted to hear, but that was too bad. It was the truth.

Phil Jorgenson at NASA was happy to let the whole thing go away. He'd never thought it was a good idea in the first place and just did it because he and Andrews were friends. But, really, an alien? In his mind, the whole thing had trouble written all over it. Time to move on. And the Onus Brothers and their sudden disappearance? Well, they were bad news from the word go. He didn't miss them at all.

For Jeremy and Ebar, the biggest issue with Ebar not going back to Rykos was his identity. And Jeremy's identity, too, for that matter. "Easily solved," Ebar said, that night around the campfire. "Just leave it to me."

Nowadays, Kyle Johnson no longer exists. Instead, all links to that former identity go to Ebar Johnson. And he has a driver's license to prove it, curtesy of some alien sleight of hand and a little laser-eye technology. Same for Jeremy Slater, who is now Walter Payton Slater, a name chosen from one of Jeremy's favorite football players. He likes his new name a lot.

Jeremy (Walt) and Ebar live in a two-bedroom apartment about a mile from Julie and Wren whom they see often. After all, their experiences together culminating with *The Incident at Cozy Cove* and the vaporization of the Onus brothers, was something that didn't occur every day. As Wren puts it, "But no matter what, it was the best thing that ever happened to us. Right Julie?"

"You bet, lover." Julie smiles whenever it comes up. She always agrees.

Upon their return from Yellowstone Park, Julie and Wren stuck around Duluth and helped Jeremy and Ebar find their own apartment. Within a few weeks after they moved in, and using his new identity as Walter Slater, Jeremy answered an ad and was immediately hired by Carlton County as a mental health counselor.

These days he's doing wonderfully. His boss is a tall, dark-skinned woman named Skylar Nelson. She was a standout basketball player at the University of Minnesota at Duluth, and she enjoys poking fun at this big, bearded Walter character whenever they go to shoot hoops together at a local gym, which is getting to be quite often. As far as she's concerned, he's not the best shot, but he's got a kind heart and is fun to be around. Skylar can see this relationship going somewhere, someplace good. And in quiet moments, when he thinks about it, which is getting to be often, so does Walter.

And Our Alien, as Julie and Wren sometimes call him? What about the alien, formally from the planet Rykos and Orchard Lake? What about him?

206

Ebar has never been happier. He's working as a lab technician at the Fresh Water Biological Institute located on the shore of Lake Superior on the north side of town, an easy ten-minute bicycle ride from Ebar and Jeremy's apartment. Well, ten minutes downhill, anyway. Nearly twenty-five minutes uphill, but that's the nature of living in Duluth on Lake Superior, and he doesn't mind it at all.

He loves his job. He does water testing for lake water pollutants and is on a team studying the effects of climate change on the big lake. He feels like it's the best job in the world, and he loves going to work every day.

Which is all well and good.

But what Ebar really loves is taking his single man kayak out on Lake Superior all by himself. He paddles along the shore and heads north of the city looking at the rocks and pine and aspen trees, enjoying the scenery and the freedom of being on the water. If the wind is right and the waves aren't too big, sometimes he paddles far out into the lake, out to where the shore is a tiny distant line on the horizon. There, he stops paddling and lets his kayak drift. He closes his eyes and becomes one with the water, one with the lake. He clears his mind and lets the currents carry him where they will. The kayak bobs along and sometimes water splashes over side, but he doesn't notice. He is enveloped by the aura of the huge lake. Time is meaningless to him. He feels the energy of Lake Superior in his entire body, nurturing him, giving him strength, making him feel not just at one with the natural world all around him, but with the entire universe. He knows there is nowhere he'd rather be. He has found the place he's been looking for his entire life.

And he is home.

About the Author

Jim lives in a small-town west of Minneapolis, Minnesota. His stories and poems have appeared in nearly four-hundred online and print publications. His collection of short stories *Resilience* was published in March 2021, by Bridge House Publishing. *Short Stuff* a collection of flash fiction and drabbles was published in October 2021, by Chapeltown Books. *Periodic Stories and Periodic Stories Volume Two* were published in July and September 2021, by Impspired. *Dreamers* a collection of short stories was published in March 2022, by Clarendon House Publishing. *Something Better* a dystopian adventure novella was published in July 2021, by Dark Myth Publications. Most recently, *Periodic Stories Volume Three – A Novel* was published in April 2022, by Impspired. His short story "Aliens" was nominated by The Zodiac Press for the 2020 Pushcart Prize. His story "The Maple Leaf" was voted 2021 story of the year for Spillwords. All of his work can be found on his blog at:
www.theviewfromlonglake.wordpress.com.

www.ingramcontent.com/pod-product-compliance
Lightning Source LLC
Chambersburg PA
CBHW061149170626
46809CB00003B/1040